Laura was a child, a six year old, little girl.
She had no idea why she'd been taken from her mummy, or where she was going.

Her new friend was nice enough, but Laura really missed her home. Luckily, she was too young to realise exactly what was about to happen to her.

Her mother was distraught. Being told that you will never see your daughter again is unimaginable. That's not something you can ever recover from.

This is a novel in the acclaimed Hedge & Cole thriller series.

Cole is a tough, ex-military man. He's the sort of person that trouble and danger seem to follow.

Hedge is a reluctant hero. Plagued with anxieties and haunted by flashbacks, he is not what you might be expecting.

It's going to be their toughest assignment yet, but getting anything close to a good outcome just doesn't seem very likely.

This is not one for the faint-hearted!

Kevin Bradley once again shows how to mix fast paced action, with suspense and intrigue. This novel will have you on the edge of your seat from start to finish.

This book would sit well alongside your Lee Child and Michael Connelly favourites!

What people are saying about The Cuba Cage

"I've read all of the books in the Hedge & Cole series now. This is one of the best! I'm not sure how you follow this one?"

"What a stunning book. I can't decide whether it reminds me of Jack Higgins, Mark Dawson or Stephen Leather. Probably a combination of all three I guess."

"This is quite a shocking book, and not for the faint-hearted. The story line covers a difficult subject. We all know that child trafficking is a wicked thing, but after reading this, you'll realise that it's much worse than that. Strong praise is due for not avoiding a terrible topic."

"I can definitely recommend this book. It's well written and will keep you gripped from start to finish. Don't expect to put it down until you reach the last page."

"What I like about this author is the fast pace and the gripping storyline. The two main characters interact well. I'm a real fan of Hedge and Cole."

"As with other books by this author, there's a touch of Lee Child about this."

About the Author

Kevin Bradley lives in England, and has travelled all over the world. He tries to bring many of his own personal observations and adventures into his novels.

The author spent all of his teenage years either at boarding school or living on military bases. The frequently exciting, and often cruel experiences from this period are clearly reflected in his writing.

Before turning to writing, Kevin had a successful business career and, as well as an Honours Degree in Social Economics, he also holds an MBA from the Edinburgh Business School.

When not writing he enjoys mountain biking and road running.

Books by Kevin Bradley

The Palindrome Cult
(Hedge & Cole / Book 1)
"A cracking good read, fast and furious, unputdownable"

The Terminate Code
(Hedge & Cole / Book 2)
"A fantastic story, breathtaking and full of intrigue, unforgettable"

The Transamerica Cell
(Hedge & Cole / Book 3)
"A gripping, tense thriller, you'll be on the edge of your seat"

The Cuba Cage
(Hedge & Cole / Book 4)
"A shockingly good novel, full of terror and suspense"

Bully Boys
(Hedge & Cole / Supplement)
"A brutal and sadistic account of boarding school life"

The Hedge & Cole Thriller Series (Books 1-4)
(Hedge & Cole / The Collection)
"A 4 book set of gripping, action adventure novels"

The Cuba Cage

Kevin Bradley

Chapter One

The man who boarded the bus was wearing a blue running vest with the Nike logo clearly displayed on its front. That in itself shouldn't have been unusual, but for the fact that he must have weighed in at well over two hundred and fifty pounds. The guy was huge, with enlarged biceps and an incredibly broad chest. From the muscle development in his legs, he looked like he worked out several days a week. But the vest must have been for comfort, as he clearly wasn't a runner.

Apart from his enormous frame, there was only one other thing that drew everyone's attention to him. He was carrying a baseball bat.

The driver of the bus eyed him suspiciously as he casually walked past. 'Hey mister, I don't want any trouble now. And I need to see your ticket.'

'I don't have a ticket. I'm not staying on, just looking for someone.'

'Like I said, I don't want trouble.' The driver pushed his reinforced glass window down, which effectively sealed off his compartment from the rest of the vehicle.

The big man tapped his bat against the glass, and smiled. The driver's hand hovered over the emergency panic button. One touch on that and the bus depot, along with the local police would be alerted, and hopefully come to provide assistance. That was the theory anyway, in practice it could be up to an hour before he might receive any kind of response.

'Don't you go touching that,' the big man grunted. Then he carried on walking down the aisle of the bus.

It was a quiet day in Gainesville, which was a reasonable size town in northern Florida. The time was around two thirty in the afternoon, and most people were either at work, in school or college, or otherwise occupied. The bus was heading downtown, and there must have been less than fifteen people on board.

As he walked down between the seats, the big man studied each of the passengers in turn. The first occupied seat he came to was on his left, and a teenage boy sat looking out of the window. He seemed nervous, as did all the other passengers. The big man tapped the youngster gently on the shoulder with the end of his bat.

'How come you're not in school today?'

The boy looked at him. There was defiance in his face, but it wasn't quite strong enough to drown out the fear clearly visible in the lad's eyes.

'My grandpa died a few days ago. I've got the afternoon off to go to the funeral.' As soon as he had spoken he turned his head back to look out of the window. He looked like he was about to cry.

'I'm sorry to hear that. That's not a nice thing to happen. My own father died when I was about your age. That's a tough break you've got there. You take care now.'

The big man lowered the bat and moved along a few rows. He stopped next to a middle-aged man with a bald head and a large, ginger coloured beard. The facial hair made him look like a Viking. He sat bolt upright in his seat with his hands resting on his knees. His arms were shaking, and he looked terrified.

'What's your name mister?'

There was no reply, just silence.

The baseball bat swung slowly upwards and came to rest softly on the man's left hand.

'I asked you a question. Please reply.'

There was a woman in the seat immediately behind. She was pale faced, with strong, brown eyes, and short cropped hair. On her knee was a young girl, maybe six or seven years old. She lifted the child off her lap and sat her down firmly in the vacant seat next to her, the one closest to the window of the bus. The woman was now sitting directly between the big man and her child. It was a protective move. When she spoke it was with a slight English accent.

'Please kindly leave this gentleman alone. He hasn't done anything to offend you. And would you get off the bus immediately, so that we may continue our journey.'

The big man turned his head slowly to stare at the woman. He didn't respond. Still holding the bat with his right hand, he moved his left hand up to his face and pushed his index finger deep inside one of his nostrils. He made a play of moving it around for a few seconds, and then pulled it out. Without looking to see if anything had stuck to the finger, he flicked it hard in the direction of the mother. She flinched briefly as she felt something soft and wet land on one side of her face.

'Disgusting animal,' she murmured and reached for a tissue from her handbag.

The man in the running vest turned back to face the Viking.

'You, get off the bus. Go and sit on that bench over there near the entrance to the park.' He used the bat to point to a nearby wooden seat.

'Why? I haven't done anything.' The man seemed terrified. He was sweating profusely.

'Get off the bus. Do it now.'

The man's face drained of its entire colour. His white complexion now contrasted heavily with his ginger beard. Slowly he stood up and walked towards the front of the bus.

Although they didn't show it, the remaining passengers were all quite relieved. The big brute had seemingly found who he was looking for, and it wasn't one of them. There was a noticeable reduction in tension on the bus.

The big man turned to face the front of the bus, watching to ensure that the Viking was getting off. His eyes kept following him as he left the bus and eventually reached the wooden bench. Then the man with the ginger beard turned and sat down.

Resting the bat on his right shoulder, the big man nodded in satisfaction. He looked to those watching him like a man who had completed a task.

But he hadn't. He had no interest in the man who looked like a Viking. That was just a bit of fun for him. A distraction.

His real target was about to become clear.

With a sudden, swift movement, he turned around swivelling on the ball of his right foot. At the same time, he swung the baseball bat towards the woman sitting next to her young daughter. With all of the power of his upper arm muscles behind it, the bat came crashing down on to her left shoulder blade. The two main bones in the area between the neck and the arm are the clavicle, or collar bone, and the scapula, the actual shoulder blade. Both of these bones completely shattered as a result of the impact of the bat.

The woman screamed in agony as she collapsed on the floor. As she fell, she instinctively tried to protect her left side with her right hand, but she was already deep in shock and so unable to fully coordinate her actions. A terrible, animal-like moaning noise was coming from her throat, as she lay in utter torment. Her left arm hung loosely by her side, now completely useless. In fact, she would never have full use of that arm again. Then the pain overwhelmed her and after just a few seconds her screams subsided, and she passed out.

With the bat resting back on his own shoulder, the big man looked around the bus. None of the other passengers had moved a muscle. In fact, not one of them was even looking in his direction. They all sat quietly, wishing that they were brave enough to intervene, but sadly realising that they weren't. Most of them were secretly pleased that the woman had gone silent, as listening to her terrible wailing had been sickening.

After nodding slowly to himself a couple of times, he turned the bat upside down and then pushed it firmly inside the belt he was wearing. Then he leaned over and plucked the small girl from her seat. Holding her tightly under one arm, he ignored her hysterical sobbing, and her frantic clawing aimed at his face. He casually stepped down from the bus, pushed his way through a crowd of pedestrians and headed off down the street.

Chapter Two

Laura was terrified.

It had all happened so fast. Firstly, the nasty man on the bus hurting her mummy. Then she had been carried away, before being bundled into a car and told to lie down quietly on the floor. After quite a long time they had arrived at a house with a big garden. The horrible, fat man had walked her up the path and knocked on the door. A slim lady with a lovely smile had taken her inside the house and given her a glass full of strawberry milkshake. And the chocolate cookies were lovely.

She had wanted to ask the lady about her mummy, but for some reason her voice no longer seemed to work. Although she was thinking things in her head, she wasn't able to speak any words. One of the things she noticed was that the slim lady talked a lot.

'Hi there Laura, you're a pretty little girl aren't you? Look at all that lovely curly hair. Now, you can call me Betty, and we are going to be good friends. How does that sound?'

Laura just looked up at the woman. Her voice still wouldn't work, but she really wanted to ask where her mummy was, and was she alright because the horrible man had hit her with a big bat.

'Now, young lady, I'm going to take you upstairs to your new bedroom. Then you can have a nice long sleep.'

Laura wasn't tired, but she followed Betty upstairs anyway. She didn't know what else to do. She was frightened. All she wanted was to go back home. It was all so confusing for her.

The bedroom didn't look very pretty. The colour blue wasn't her favourite. She wanted to ask why she couldn't have a yellow bedroom, like the one she had in her real home, but the words wouldn't come out of her mouth properly.

There was a small, brown teddy bear lying on the bed, and she reached across and picked it up. It smelt funny, not like her bear Boris, or even like Amelia, her dolly. But it was a cute looking bear, so she hung on to it anyway.

The lady was watching her. 'Yes, that's for you. I thought you'd like it. What shall we call him?'

Laura just shook her head. She didn't know what to call him. Her mummy would know. She was good at things like that. But where was she? Maybe she had been taken to the hospital. She had shouted out very loud when the horrible man had hit her.

Betty was opening the door to another room. As she did so, she turned back towards the child.

'This is the washroom. Let's get you ready for bed, and then we can all look forward to an exciting day tomorrow.'

Just as she was climbing into the bed, Betty sat down next to her. She smiled softly and explained that Laura needed to take some medicine.

'But I'm not poorly,' the little girl thought to herself. She tried to move away from the woman.

Betty took hold of her by the arm. 'This is nice medicine. It will make you sleep really well. You'll like it as it tastes like strawberry ice cream.'

Laura didn't look convinced, but she swallowed a large spoonful of the sweet liquid. The lady was right, it did taste of strawberries. And it did make her tired. She felt drowsy almost immediately, and a few minutes later she was fast asleep.

Laura slept well, but she had some horrible dreams. She held on to her new bear hoping that the bad things would go away.

In one of the dreams a man with small, wiry spectacles was holding her arm tightly. There was a humming machine with a big needle in one of his hands and he was pushing it really hard into the top of one of her arms. It hurt a lot, and she wanted to scream. Her arm felt a bit numb for a while, and then the dream disappeared.

The next thing that she was imagining was being carried outside. It was dark, and quite cold. The wind was blowing and she felt it on her skin. It made her shiver. Betty was smiling down at her, and trying to take her new bear away. Laura tried to hold on to him, but she felt a little rip and the bear's head started to come loose. In the end she had to let go of him, otherwise his head would have come off completely.

It was the last part of her dream that was most horrible. She guessed that actually this was what people called a nightmare, as she felt herself being pushed through a small hole in the top of a wooden box. For some reason the box had felt a bit like a prison, but she hadn't done anything wrong, had she? It was only bad people who went to jail. Why was she being locked up?

Then a terrible thought occurred to her. She should have helped her mummy when she had been attacked by the bad man. But she hadn't been able to, she was too scared, and he was much too strong. That was probably why she was being put in prison. Why hadn't she helped her mummy?

'I'm sorry mummy, really sorry,' she thought to herself.

And then the lid of the box was put back in place.

In the dream she imagined herself shut away in the dark.

And she realised that she was all alone.

Chapter Three

The tattooist hated working on small girls.

Somehow boys didn't bother him. They would all grow up into horrible teenagers in the near future. And he disliked teenagers. They were nasty, ill-mannered little people. Perhaps there were some good ones, but he hadn't met many.

The girl was fast asleep. Actually she was unconscious. He knew the handlers drugged them somehow, but he didn't ask any questions.

The job he had been given was straightforward enough, but that still didn't mean he had to enjoy it. If only he could resist the lure of the casino. It was hard to imagine that he had amassed debts of over thirty thousand dollars, but that was apparently what it was. And the interest rate was exorbitant, but you didn't argue with those kinds of people.

The manager of the casino had agreed to let him pay it off in lumps, as long as it was all settled up in the next twelve months. He really didn't want to think about what would happen if he didn't do that. Although the gambling den he frequented looked smart and upmarket, the people who ran it acted more like gangsters. They were brutes. At one point a colour photograph was put in front of him showing a man lying in the dirt. Both of the man's feet had been cut off, and the stubs were black and charred. It had been explained to him how a hot iron had been used to stop the blood loss from the limbs, and seal the nerve endings. Quite a painful process apparently, especially without anaesthetic.

The tattooist was desperate to keep all of his limbs fully functioning, so it was important that he paid off the debts within the required time.

So doing the work for the man from Cuba had become essential. It paid very well. Not only was he slowly clearing the debt, but he could also afford to keep gambling. In fact, he had been doing very well recently. Just last month he had almost won fifteen hundred dollars on the roulette wheel. It was so close. He had picked the number five, and the ball had settled into the number six slot. How close can you get? He had finished the month just three thousand dollars down. Yes, his luck was definitely changing for the better.

The girl seated in front of him was six years old. He knew that from her birthday. He wiped some clear antiseptic lotion across the top of her arm, dried it off with a clean paper tissue, and then he went to work. The needle of the tattoo machine buzzed softly as firstly, he carefully inked into her arm the eight numerals that made up her date of birth.

Once completed, he looked down at the booklet he'd been given. It was important not to make any mistakes. Although he had done this kind of job many times before, he still checked the order in which he was required to do things.

Underneath the first line, in similar small numerals, and with the same black ink, he wrote the number '1058'. He glanced down at his handbook, and then moving down her arm a fraction of an inch, directly under the previous numbers he inked 'O-NEG'.

The next line in the booklet stated 'WBC7200' and the one after that read 'RBC4.9.' Using the tattoo machine, he wrote these on the girl's arm. After three more lines of inking he was finished. He carefully wiped the top of the girl's arm again with the antiseptic lotion, and then placed a clean bandage over the fresh tattoo.

'All done,' he said to the lady who called herself Betty.

'Good. I will arrange for the usual payment to be made,' she replied.

After packing away his equipment, he quickly left and hoped that he would be home in time to get some dinner. He had told his wife that he wouldn't be too late. With a bit of luck she would want one of her usual early nights. Then, once she had trundled off to bed, he could get down the casino for a couple of hours before they closed.

It felt like one of those nights when a big win was almost a certainty.

Chapter Four

Ruby Anderson wasn't a bad person. She just preferred the finer things in life. Although her husband had moved out of their apartment about eight months ago, she wasn't lonely or unhappy. Her lifestyle was good, and she had a wide circle of friends. It was just a shame that she didn't have more disposable income.

The job she had in the records office of the South Gainesville Medical Center paid reasonably well. Certainly not enough, but then she couldn't expect a lot else as she wasn't particularly well qualified. She had tried to study at school, but it didn't come naturally, and there were too many other distractions. The trouble was that dining out in lovely restaurants, having good quality clothes, and the odd piece of jewellery all meant spending money. And after all, didn't she deserve it? Having to put up with a cheating husband for nearly two years hadn't been easy.

It was only eleven o'clock in the morning but already she had logged in to her bank account three times now to check her online statement. She clicked on the balance summary. It showed a total in the account of just over five thousand dollars.

'Yes, at last,' she exclaimed with delight.

It had been three days ago that she'd passed a photocopy of the young girl's medical records to the man wearing the long raincoat. They had met at a bar just around the corner from where she worked. She immediately noticed his coat, and had pointed out to him that there was no rain forecast that day. He had ignored the remark, and reminded her that she was to tell no one about the transaction.

'No one,' she had nodded in agreement.

It was an easy five grand. All she had done was to check through the records of all the young females in the Gainesville area and matched the requirements to those she had been given. Sifting through files on her desktop computer was what she did every day, so no one would suspect her of any malpractice. The main hospital database contained around fifty thousand personal files, so she wrote a small search algorithm in order to narrow down the number of records. The whole thing had taken her less than three hours. Yes, it was an easy five thousand dollars.

The man in the raincoat had said he needed the information for research purposes, but he couldn't go via normal channels as the company he represented had been infiltrated by industrial spies. The medical trials business is worth billions of dollars, so his explanation had sounded plausible. Anyway, no one was getting hurt. So she was comfortable with herself.

The girl in the folder she had handed over was called Laura. She was six years old and the home address was that of a pleasant area on the edge of Gainesville. The dossier contained all of her medical history and personal information. The man had flicked through the file quickly and said that it looked very good. The child appeared to fit his requirements perfectly. He knew exactly what he was looking for and he could tell that she was in an excellent state of health. Telling Ruby that she had done well, he advised her that the cash would be paid very soon.

Now that the money had been deposited, Ruby would be able to confirm the holiday she had planned with two of her friends. The Bahamas would be lovely at this time of year, and she had always wanted to learn to scuba dive. She couldn't contain herself any longer. Picking up her cell phone, she clicked on the number for the travel agent.

Chapter Five

The man walking towards the gantry crane was slightly overweight, mainly because he loved his food. He couldn't resist a well made pizza. Ham and pineapple was his favourite, although a good spicy sausage on a thin crusty base came a close second.

Today though, he wasn't concerned about that, he had too many other things on his mind. His skull was throbbing with a massive headache. That was mainly as a result of the whole bottle of vodka he had drunk at around one o'clock earlier that same morning. After that he had passed out. When he awoke, he had found himself scrunched up on the back seat of his car, which had been parked on a piece of waste ground not far from where he worked.

He had then driven for almost a mile following the signs for the port of Miami which was situated in the Biscayne Bay area of the city. The port is able to boast that it handles more passengers than any other in the world. It is also one of the largest cargo ports in the entire United States. It employed a lot of people, and he was one of them. He had worked there for many years, an 'old hand' as people would say.

As he walked into an untidy looking, metal-clad building, his foreman shouted out a friendly greeting. 'Good morning Steve or judging by the look of you, a bad night.' He let out a loud belly laugh. Several other men in the building turned to see what was so funny.

Steve held up his hand in response, but said nothing. His head was still pounding, and he needed to get to the washroom urgently.

The foreman was still laughing. 'Get yourself over to gantry number three as soon as you can. I want to get that boat going to Havana loaded up and under way within the next hour.'

Again Steve said nothing. Instead he gave the thumbs up sign with his right hand and disappeared behind a white door marked Staff Only.

Once inside the washroom, he locked himself in a toilet cubicle, and began to cry. The pain in his head was excruciating. He wasn't a big drinker, so the bottle of cheap vodka had caused him a lot of damage. But that wasn't the main reason he was so distraught. It was what he had witnessed earlier in the evening that had left him so bereft. What was she thinking of? They had been together now for over eight years. He thought he trusted her. He had hoped that they were a team.

Although they had never married, Teresa was the love of his life. He knew she had a voracious sexual appetite, but hadn't he matched her every step of the way?

They had gone out early the previous evening to a party. One of his work colleagues was celebrating the birth of their first child. Steve knew most of the people there, and Teresa seemed to be enjoying herself. He always smiled to himself when he thought of her surrounded by his friends. Well, she was an attractive woman. Her Spanish heritage had given her a broad smile, and long black hair. She also had large baby-blue eyes, which she could use to considerable effect.

It was still early, around nine o'clock, when she said she wasn't feeling too good and was going to head home. Insisting that he should stay and enjoy himself, she had then called a taxi. Steve had initially agreed to stay, but forty five minutes later he started to feel guilty about Teresa being on her own at home, particularly as she was unwell. So he also gave his apologies and left the party.

Arriving home, he let himself in by the front door, and started walking upstairs. He wanted to surprise her, although he thought that his girlfriend would by now be fast asleep. As he approached the bedroom though, he realised that something wasn't right. There were clothes scattered on the floor near the bedroom door, and loud noises were coming from the room.

The door was open slightly, with around a six inch gap, and he used this to see what was going on in the room. What he saw took his breath away. Teresa was kneeling on the bed, completely naked. A man who Steve didn't recognise was standing next to the bed in front of her. He was also fully undressed, and his erect penis was sticking out in front of him. Steve couldn't see all of it though, as most of it was in his girlfriend's mouth. The man had his head thrown back and was moaning softly as he slowly moved backwards and forwards, pushing his shaft deep into Teresa's throat.

Steve was about to burst into the room and demand to know what the hell was going on, but he stopped suddenly when he saw the second man. His shirt had been removed, but he still had his boxer shorts on. He was lying underneath Teresa, with his back on the bed, and somehow he had pushed her breasts together and was sucking both of her nipples at the same time. Steve could clearly hear her groans of pleasure as the man her feasted on her breasts.

It was too much to bear, and Steve closed his eyes while he pondered what the hell he should do. How could she do this to him? Surely he didn't deserve to be cheated on like this. In the last few seconds his whole world seemed to have come crashing in on him. His eyes flicked open again when he suddenly heard a loud grunting noise. Pushing his head against the door, and looking to the left side of the bed, he now spotted the third man, who was also fully naked. He was thrusting himself hard against Teresa's buttocks, and Steve realised with some horror that the man's penis must be deep inside his beloved girlfriend. As he continued watching, the man's thrusts increased their pace, and then, suddenly he let out a long ecstatic scream and pushed himself one last time deep into Teresa. Now that he had reached his climax the man's movements ceased, and he rested himself against her back, trying to get his breathing to return to normal.

Steve had seen enough. He couldn't take any more. Leaving the house quickly, he ran to his car and sat slumped in the driver's seat for several minutes. His mind was spinning, and he was sweating profusely. He was struggling to control his emotions. There had been genuine love between the two of them. They had told each other as much on many occasions. Why had she needed to cheat on him? Wasn't he enough for her?

There were too many questions spinning about in his head, but no answers. Placing the key in the ignition, he started the car and sped away. He couldn't remember where he went, or for how long. Neither did he recall where he had bought the bottle of vodka.

All he could remember was the pain.

He was still sitting in the toilet cubicle when he heard some voices outside. Two of his fellow workers had entered the washroom. Wiping his eyes with some toilet tissue, he waited for the men to leave. He didn't want to walk out and let them see him looking like he had been crying. He would never live it down.

Eventually the men left. He gave them a couple of minutes, and then followed them out of the washroom. Keeping his head down, he quickly made his way out of the building and headed towards gantry three as requested. He felt like shit and wasn't sure how he was going to make it through the day. His head was spinning and his eyesight was blurred. The best thing to do was just to get on with what he needed to do as quickly as possible.

If only he could get the sickening images of the three men and his girlfriend out of his head.

Chapter Six

There were six crates for Marco to inspect that morning. That was about normal he thought to himself as he approached the dockside. The most he had ever seen loaded onto a single boat was eleven. But occasionally there had been as few as two. It was the same routine every Wednesday, and he knew exactly what he had to do. It wasn't a difficult job, but many people wouldn't have done it. The money was very good though, too good. And Marco's uncle, who was based in Havana, paid regularly and without any fuss.

Marco looked South American. His dark skin and well defined cheekbone structure gave him the appearance of a Columbian. But he and the rest of his family were actually from Cuba. Most of them worked for his uncle Jorge, who owned several boats. The one being loaded today was one of his fleet. The vessel looked untidy, and was desperately in need of some maintenance. It had been painted a nondescript dark brown colour, except for the small enclosed bridge at the back of the boat, which for some unknown reason, was coloured bright yellow. The vessel wasn't very big, but it was large enough to carry the crates that were loaded into its hull on the third working day of each week.

Marco approached the first crate. It was exactly four feet high. The width and depth were also the same measurement, so it formed a perfect cube. All the crates were the same size. The timber was a pale colour and had rough edges. Marco thought it was probably some kind of sawn pine, but he wasn't sure. He was no wood expert. In fact he knew very little about anything. Most of his life had been spent drifting from one job to another. That was until two years ago when his uncle had appointed him Chief Export

Inspector for his shipping business. Marco was based in Miami. He had his accommodation and living expenses all paid for by the company, and he received a payment transfer direct to his bank account on the last day of every month. Yes, he had certainly landed on his feet, at last.

As he walked up to the first wooden box, he pulled a bunch of keys out from his jacket pocket. On top of each crate was a locked, wooden flap, about two feet wide and eighteen inches deep. Each of the locks was colour coded so that it could easily be matched up with its respective key. This lock had a black tag on it, so Marco quickly found the black key in his bunch and pushed it into the locking mechanism. The padlock clicked open, and Marco's eyes flashed nervously around, before he lifted the inspection flap.

The interior of the crate was pitch black. Marco had already pulled out his rubber coated flashlight and clicked it on. Instantly a strong beam of light illuminated the entire area inside the box. The first thing that any onlooker would have noticed was that inside the wooden crate were steel bars. They ran along the entire inside surface of the box, each bar separated from the next by a distance of four inches. In fact the steel formed a complete structure of its own. Therefore, if all of the wood was removed from the exterior of the crate, what was left would be a steel cage.

As each crate was a four foot cube, the total inside area was around sixty four cubic feet. Most of this space was unused. Using the metric system of measurement, a person weighing eighty kilograms would occupy around eighty liters of space. The small girl lying at the bottom of this crate probably weighed only around fifty kilograms. So she would have occupied around fifty liters of space, which is less than three cubic feet.

Marco leaned further over the inspection flap so that he could get a better look. As usual the smell from inside the crate hit him immediately. It was a combination of stale sweat, fresh urine, and human excrement. He coughed as the stench hit his nostrils, and backed away briefly. He took a deep breath and then leaned his head back over the hole.

Marco settled the beam of his torch on the girl. She lay still, unconscious from the drugs that had been pumped into her body a short while earlier. There was a thick blanket underneath her body, which gave some comfort from the cold steel bars that covered the bottom of the crate. The girl looked to be about six years old, with a pale white face. She had a bandage around the top of her arm. That was quite normal though, Marco had seen that many times before. As he checked the girl to make sure she was still breathing, Marco felt a surge of pity. Then as quickly as that emotion had arrived, he pushed it away. He had a job to do, and his wife and children depended on him. He locked the crate back up, and moved along the quayside to the next one.

All of the first five crates were fine. He ensured they were all locked correctly, and that they were all occupied. The occupants were to be confirmed as unconscious, but breathing easily. It was important that they arrived alive and uninjured. If not, the cargo was worthless, and the transportation costs would have been wasted. There would certainly be no refunds of the large amounts of cash it took to ensure that the port officials didn't inspect the manifest too closely.

As soon as he had opened the last of the crates, Marco knew that he had a massive problem. The girl inside the crate was not fully unconscious. Although she was lying on the floor of the cage, her head was moving slightly and she was moaning. The noises she was making weren't loud, but if she was heard by anyone on the quay, then there would be trouble.

He had experienced this situation a few times in the past. He cursed the handlers further down the operation for not doing their jobs properly. Either they hadn't administered the correct drug dosages, or they couldn't be bothered to check that the drugs had worked properly. Anyhow, it was now his problem. He had to get on with the loading as quickly as possible, and this last crate had be dealt with first.

He walked off urgently to find the loading officer in charge of this section of the port.

Chapter Seven

Steve was heading in the direction of gantry number three, when a dark-skinned man approached him.

'Are you the guy loading my boat this morning?' Marco stared at him with a look of surprise on his face. The man looked unwell, and seemed to be walking as if he was drunk, or maybe even on drugs.

'Yes, I'm heading over that way now. I'll start loading up in a few minutes.'

Marco nodded back at him. 'Thanks, that's great. Let me show you which crate I need you to load first. By the way, are you okay? You look like shit.'

'I'm fine,' Steve lied. 'I had a difficult night, and didn't sleep much. But I'm okay. Let's go and get your boat loaded.'

Steve took another headache pill from his near empty packet. The images of what he had witnessed the previous evening were still flashing across his mind. The alcohol had worked briefly, and for most of the night the memory of the three men abusing his woman had been erased. But now those visions had returned, and they swarmed around inside his head like angry bees. He drew his hand across his face and wiped away another tear, as a picture of Teresa's smiling face pierced his mind. She had clearly been enjoying the experience immensely, her ecstasy was obvious.

His thoughts were interrupted as the dark-skinned man he had met on the quayside a few moments ago was now shouting something at him.

'This one first please.' The man was pointing at a wooden crate on the end of a line of six identical crates. 'Are you hearing me mister? This is the first one I need loaded. Let's get on with this. I need to get this boat moving.'

Steve nodded at the man, and then started to climb the steps up to the cab on the crane. The guy on the quay below was annoying him. He seemed stressed out by something.

'Screw him,' he muttered to himself. 'He thinks he's got problems. He'll just have to wait until I'm good and ready.'

Steve took his time settling into his cab. The pill he had taken a few moments ago had managed to lodge itself in his throat, so he took a bottle of water from his rucksack and swallowed a few gulps. Normally his lunch bag would contain his flask of hot coffee, and a home-made meat pie. Not today though. This day wasn't what he would call a normal day.

The man below the gantry was still standing near one of the crates. He was waving his arms up and down, and then pointing at the wooden box.

'Okay, calm down you bloody idiot,' Steve muttered to himself.

He pressed the starter button on the crane, and instantly the electric motor whirred into life. He moved his control levers carefully, until they closed in on the crate at the end of the line below him. His vision was still badly blurred, and his concentration was off, but he had done this operation a thousand times before. It wouldn't be a problem. Vivid images of his naked girlfriend were still racing around in his head. He tried to ignore them, so that he could focus on the job. It wasn't easy.

Marco watched as the crane picked up the first crate.

'Hey, go careful, that's valuable goods in this cargo, for Christ sake.'

He could see the crane operator sitting behind his controls. The guy still looked unwell. Marco had him down as an alcoholic. The man's breath had reeked of drink when he had spoken to him earlier. The crate was now being lifted off the concrete quay, and the gantry had started to swing it towards the boat. The large doors which sealed the cargo hold of the boat were wide open. The crates were small in comparison to most of the containers and other cargo that the port handled. It was a relatively easy job to gently position the boxes inside the hold of the ship.

The arm of the crane that had clamped onto the crate was now moving towards the rear of the ship. It was moving with a jerky motion, making it look like the operator was some kind of novice. Each time the arm of the crane stuttered, the load being carried dropped further, a little more into an acute angle. By the time the crate had reached the edge of the quay, it was being held in a very precarious way.

'What the hell are you doing? Straighten it out man.' Marco was shouting at the top of his voice. He was getting worried. This guy seemed like he had no idea what he was supposed to be doing. 'You're losing your grip on it. Swing it back towards the quay. What the hell?'

Steve couldn't hear him. Sitting up in the cab tears had once again started to sting his eyes. 'What a bitch,' he kept mumbling to himself. He was repeating the same phrase over and over again. 'What a bitch.'

His vision was fuzzy, and his hands were shaking badly. He looked across at the arm of the crane. The crate he was moving had disappeared from his sight. He remembered it being positioned near the boat. It must now be inside the vessel's hold. But he couldn't remember moving his lever down.

'Oh well, damn it, it's only a crate, probably full of some crap. Under ripe tomatoes, crappy cotton shirts for overweight men, or some cheap tobacco substitute for those expensive Cuban cigars,' he muttered to himself.

Then he pressed the release button on his console in front of him, hoping that the box was where it should be in the ship's hold.

It wasn't.

Not even close.

It hit the surface of the sea about three yards from the back of the boat, and within a few seconds it had completely disappeared below the gentle swell.

Chapter Eight

Abigail Green was frightened.

She had only a hazy recollection of events from the last few days. Her head was spinning, and she felt nauseous. The thick, woollen blanket she was lying on was already wet as a result of her needing to urinate earlier in the day. It hadn't helped when she had thrown up on it as well. She vaguely recalled feeling sick as a result of the box she was in being moved around.

Although she was lying on the blanket, the surface underneath her seemed like a series of metal bars. It was impossible to see anything though, as the inside of her small prison was completely dark. For a split second, when the beam of light had shined close to her a short while ago, the container she was in looked like a metal cage, enclosed in some kind of box.

It seemed like a long time had passed since she'd been walking home from school. She lived with her parents in a pleasant area of Orlando. Her father ran a busy building equipment rental business, based on the outskirts of the city. Although Abigail was only nine years old, her mother allowed her to walk the last four hundred yards from the school bus stop to the family house.

She started to cry again as she remembered the black van that had pulled up next to her, and the fat man who had grabbed her roughly by the arm and pulled her inside the vehicle. Her school bag had been ripped from her hand, and thrown into a nearby hedge. That had worried her. There were several expensive school workbooks in the bag. Her mum would have to pay for them if they weren't recovered, or became damaged.

She felt like she had been drugged, although she wasn't exactly sure how that was supposed to feel. Once, at a party her parents had given for her father's top employees, she had drunk two glasses of red wine. The taste was sour, she recalled, but the light headed feeling she had been left with was quite a pleasant sensation.

The box she was in moved suddenly and she screamed. It felt like she was being lifted upwards, and then sideways. With the small amount of strength she had left she tried to bang on the side wall, but she caught her knuckles on a metal bar and it hurt. Tears were rolling down her face now. She really needed to go to the toilet, but it was bad enough wetting herself. Anything more than that would just be disgusting.

'Help me please. Mummy, help,' she cried.

Now she was sobbing uncontrollably. Lying back down on the blanket, she shut her eyes tightly. Then, suddenly, she was falling. It felt like someone had dropped the box she was in. A split second later it landed on what seemed like a hard surface. She was confused though, as she thought that she heard a splash of water. The cage she was in settled at a strange angle, and she fell down between two sides of the box.

'Oh my god, what's happening,' she screamed.

To her horror, she suddenly realised that the box was rapidly filling up with water. Already her legs were submerged, and the level was rising fast. The water on her skin felt incredibly cold, in contrast to the heat that had built up inside the crate. She started to scream as loud as she could, and once more tried to bang on the side of the wooden box. As her hand struck the surface though, she recoiled and screeched in pain. The arm that had struck the wood felt like it was on fire, and an agonising jolt ran down the whole of her forearm. What she didn't know was that the arm had banged hard against the metal bars of the cage as it had struck the surface of the water, and the bone in her forearm had been badly fractured.

The water level was now up to her neck, and she was crying hysterically. She couldn't shout out any more as she had no energy left, and anyway the cold water was making her shiver uncontrollably.

There was only a few inches of air left in the top of the crate now, and she turned her head upwards so that her mouth could suck it in. Her last thoughts were of her mother, and how worried she would be when she hadn't turned up from school that day.

Then the air was gone, and the water had replaced it. It didn't matter how hard she breathed in, there was no air left.

Only water.

On the side of the quay Marco was furious. He was waving his fist at the crane operator above him, and swearing profusely. The loss of the cargo was serious, and he would be in trouble for it. The costs would almost certainly be deducted from his monthly payment. His uncle was a reasonable person, but he didn't appreciate failure. Jorge was not a man to disappoint. He ran his operation with an iron fist. Marco had personally witnessed the brutal execution of a man who had withheld cash from his uncle. The poor guy had been pushed off the top of a ten-storey building. A handsome pay-off to the Havana police chief resulted in a verdict of suicide. No, Uncle Jorge was not someone to be messed with.

Marco peered over the side of the quay to see if he could spot the crate. It must have sunk immediately, as it was nowhere in sight. The tides in this area are quite strong, so hopefully it would be washed out to sea. He had no choice but to forget about it, he was hardly going to report the missing cargo to the port authorities.

Marco cursed one more time, and then walked off to see if he could find a replacement crane operator. The guy behind the controls at the moment was a drunken idiot. It was important that he got the remaining crates loaded as fast as possible. The journey to Havana was just the start. From there, each of the wooden boxes would be sent on to their final destinations all over the world. These were all specially ordered specimens. Any delay could seriously impact the quality of the delivered product. Some of the crates had to be on connecting flights. Timing was critical.

Marco cursed to himself again. 'Time is money as they say,' he muttered angrily to himself.

Chapter Nine

Maddie stood with her brother looking out over the side of the cruise ship. It was a beautiful day, and the Caribbean Sea was calm. The sun was high up in a perfectly cloudless sky, and the temperature was well into the nineties. This was the third day of their trip, and they had already visited Jamaica and the Cayman Islands.

'There are worse places to be.' Hedge looked across at his sister. She was smiling brightly, and her blue eyes looked full of life. The wind was light, but there was enough of it to blow her long, blonde hair back across her shoulders.

She glanced towards him. 'I can't think of many better places right now. It's perfect. I'm really looking forward to seeing Havana. I've heard it's charming.'

'Well you haven't got long to wait. I can see the island of Cuba in the distance. We should be docking there within the next couple of hours.'

She put her arm around his shoulders. It was a sign of how content she was. They carried on looking out across the sea as a few hundred yards away a small cargo boat slowly moved past them. It looked a bit drab and rusty, and in need of a paint job, Hedge thought. It was hard not to miss the wheelhouse at the back of the boat, as the sunlight reflected sharply off the bright yellow paintwork.

As it was such a pleasant day, there were many other passengers lining the railings on this side of the ship, all staring out across the pale blue sea. Hedge ran his eyes down the side of the boat, taking in the various groups of people. Immediately in front of him and his sister were an elderly couple. They had been waving frantically at the cargo boat as it had passed, hoping that someone on board the small vessel might have waved back. No one did.

Next to the elderly couple were a group of young women, chatting together excitedly. They seemed to all have American accents, so he assumed they were college or work friends spending a week cruising through the Caribbean. Beyond this group was a young couple, standing close together arm in arm as they looked out over the calm sea.

A family group were next in line on the ships railings. There were seven of them altogether, two grandparents, a mother and father, and three children. All related, Hedge guessed, but he didn't know for sure. They all huddled closely together, chatting constantly. Two of the youngsters were boys, maybe twins as they appeared very similar, and they were shouting noisily and pushing into each other. They looked to be around seven or eight years old. Hedge smiled to himself. They were typical boys messing about.

The third child was a young girl, aged around five maybe. She was hanging onto her father's back, with her arms around his neck. She was looking down, watching her older brothers misbehaving, and laughing at them as they did so.

Maddie had stopped looking out at the distant horizon, and was now staring in the direction of the two boys and their sister. If anyone had been watching her, they would have said that she had a quizzical, faraway look in her eyes. Her normal breathing pattern had changed and was now quite shallow, and her lips had turned a light shade of blue.

She squeezed her brother's shoulder a little tighter, and without looking at him she said 'take your sunglasses off.'

'Why?' he said, slightly surprised by her request. 'It's so bright out here. Anyway, why are you suddenly acting so serious?'

'Take your glasses off and pass them to me, and then take your sandals off,' she said quietly.

He looked around at her. He was about to ask why again, but he stared into her face, and for some reason he decided not to. She had a strange look about her, and her eyes appeared dull and lifeless. Her expression was extremely serious. He wasn't entirely sure why he followed her instructions, but he removed his sunglasses and handed them to her. Then he leaned down and pulled off both of his sandals. He looked back at her as if now expecting an explanation for her strange requests.

She was staring at the family group with an expression of pure terror in her eyes.

Hedge followed her gaze, and as he did so, he saw that the two boys were now wrestling on the deck. Their previous horseplay had turned into a full scale brawl. The father had swivelled around towards the boys, and was trying to break up the fight. The young girl, still on her father's back, now found herself right next to the wooden railing of the ship. Before any of the adults could react, she had let go of her father's neck and had hopped onto the railing. She was laughing as she balanced on the four inch wide strip of wood.

The young girl's father suddenly realised that her weight was no longer pulling on his neck. He turned to see where she was, and was horrified to realise that she was perched precariously on the railing.

'Emily, grab hold of me please,' he shouted to her.

He reached out towards the child, but as he did so she laughed mischievously, and arched her body away from him playfully in order to avoid his hand. As she leaned backwards, her feet slipped on the glossy, wooden surface.

She screamed as she tumbled out beyond the railing, and fell sixty feet into the sea below.

Chapter Ten

The ship was moving gently through the water at what seemed like a good speed, but was still only travelling at around ten miles an hour. That equates to something like fourteen feet per second. The point where Emily had fallen overboard was about two hundred feet from the back of the vessel. That meant that after fifteen seconds or so, the young girl would have been behind the back of the boat, stranded in the Caribbean Sea.

Hedge of course, had not calculated this fifteen second window with that kind of accuracy. He had simply reacted without hesitation. He started running down the deck towards the back of the boat, not sure exactly what his next move was going to be.

As he ran he could hear the screaming of the mother behind him. 'Emily ….. my baby…… someone help….. stop the boat …please help.'

Other women along the deck had also started screaming as they saw the young girl drifting by in the water below. Several people had begun to move towards the back of the boat, although it looked to Hedge like this was just curiosity, rather than any obvious intent to help in any way.

'Out of my way,' he shouted, as he ran past the other passengers.

Hedge sensed that he was keeping pace with the girl in the water as he ran. He couldn't see Emily, as she would be too close to the ship, but he could see some of the passengers indicating her position in the water as he hurtled past them.

The rear of the boat was approaching fast. He would be at the back railing in a few more seconds.

'How did she know?' he said to himself under his breath. Maddie had told him to take off his sunglasses and shoes, almost as if she knew something was about to happen. Had it been in readiness for this situation? How could she possibly have known?

He had to make a quick decision as he reached the back of the boat. There was no sign of any other rescue option and so it appeared to be down to him. He slowed his pace down and he jumped up onto the wooden railing. His momentum carried him forward, and so he stood on the railing for just a second, before his body started to lean towards the rear of the boat. He couldn't stop himself. He was committed to letting his body fall into the sea below.

Just at that split second though, he looked down from the railing, and expected to see the seawater beneath him. He instantly realised he had a problem. The surface of the sea was not immediately underneath him. Thirty feet below was another deck. This deck didn't exist at the sides, which is why the girl had fallen directly into the sea. At the back, however, it extended for about fifteen feet beyond the upper deck he had been standing on.

He was committed to diving off the back though, so he had to push off from the railing with all the strength his legs could muster in order to clear the railing at the back of the lower deck. It was fortunate he had taken off his sandals, as with them still on he would have found no purchase on the wet railing. His bare feet, however, didn't slide on the wooden surface and so he could get maximum push off towards the rear of the boat.

'But how did she know?' he thought to himself again.

He was now diving through the air towards the rear railing on the lower deck. It is amazing how rapidly the human brain can think in a crisis, and so it was that his mind started to discuss the concept of momentum. He tried to reason that as the boat was moving, it would help him to clear the railing below. Not true, his brain contradicted itself, he had been standing on the boat and so he also had forward momentum, which would cancel the effect of the boat moving underneath him. He tried to ignore this argument and focus on clearing the wooden beam that was fast approaching. He was now just a few feet away and he tried desperately to arch his back to loop his body over.

Then his head was over the railing, next his body moved past it, and finally he tried to flick his feet over. His right foot missed the wooden beam by a fraction of an inch, but his left foot hit it as it passed. There wasn't much contact, but it was enough to send a spasm of pain running down his leg. He didn't realise it at the time, but the impact had broken three of his toes, and bent the foot back with such force that it had ripped several small tendons in the lower half of his leg.

This only troubled him for a moment, as he had now hit the surface of the water and was immediately surprised by how cold it was. Although the Caribbean islands are surrounded by warm waters, out in the middle of the sea the temperatures decline as the depth of water increases. Whilst certainly not as cold as the Atlantic, water temperatures of sixty five degrees Fahrenheit are possible. This is considerably colder than many indoor swimming pools.

The human body has an excellent built in system for preservation should it ever find itself accidentally thrust into cold water. Within seconds, all the blood supply is redistributed by the brain so that it focuses on keeping warm the core parts of the body such as the heart, and other vital organs. Heat is moved away from extremities, such as hands and feet, as these are deemed not to be critical for life preservation. Worse than that however, that the body increases its breathing rate rapidly in order to maintain an adequate oxygen supply to the lungs. This leaves the unfortunate person in the position of having to gasp for air several times a second, which is fine if you are on the surface of the water. Hedge was reacting to the cold water, but he was now some four or five metres under the surface. His body started to gasp for air, resulting in him taking in a few mouthfuls of salty water.

He swam quickly upwards towards the light. On reaching the surface he gasped down several huge mouthfuls of air.

How could it be this cold? He thought to himself. It's the bloody Caribbean, not exactly the Arctic Sea, although to him it certainly felt like it. He started to shiver. Was it the water or was he scared? He pushed the thought away and tried to focus his mind. It was very frightening bobbing around in the water, especially as the ship he had been on a few moments earlier was fast pulling away from him.

The water he had swallowed was causing him to choke again. He felt like he was suffocating as he hadn't been able to get enough air into his lungs, and the salt in the water was making him gag. He felt sick, panicky and disorientated.

He tried to pull himself together. He needed to focus. Where was the girl? He remembered her name.

'Emily, Emily,' he called out desperately.

He looked around him, but he could see nothing but water in all directions. The sea had looked calm from sixty feet up, but now it felt choppy, with waves climbing several feet over his head. He tried to get his bearings. The ship was disappearing into the distance, so he knew which direction he had started from.

He thought that the vessel would surely turn and come back and pick them up, but he dismissed the idea instantly. A ship that size is going to take at least thirty minutes to slow down, turn, and then come back. If he didn't manage to find her, the girl would surely be dead by then, he thought.

He looked once more towards the ship. There were many people standing looking back at him in the water. It was difficult for him to make out any detail, but he thought he could see a tall figure at one end of the crowd, with his hand up, pointing to Hedge's left. Was that person trying to tell him something?

He started swimming in that direction. He swam for what he thought was twenty feet. It was slow going as he was starting to feel cold, and shaking violently with fear. He also had to keep stopping to clear his mouth and throat of sea water. He ceased swimming for a moment and looked back at the boat. There was the dark figure again, more distant now, but pointing back behind him. Hedge set off again, another twenty feet of swimming. Again he stopped and looked for the dark figure on the boat. He could barely make it out, but as he focused his eyes, he felt sure that the figure had his hand held out with a 'thumbs up' signal.

Hedge looked around him. 'Emily, Emily,' he shouted.

He spun in the water, going round several times. Then, he saw splashing, and a head bobbed up from below the surface.

'Help…. Help ….. I'm drowning….. I can't swim,' a child's voice cried out.

He instantly swam towards the desperate shout. He could see a small head in the water, but as he got close, it dropped once more beneath the waves. He ducked his own head down below the surface of the sea. He felt so cold. His hands had started to go numb, and his feet ached, particularly the left one. Every time he kicked with it, a needle like pain shot through his body.

'How did she know?' The thought came back to him again. Don't worry about it now though, stay focused. It's so cold though.

Swimming underwater for what seemed an age, his hand caught hold of something. It felt like hair. He pulled it to him, and then he was holding the girl. He swam for the surface, pulling her with him. Finally he was able to breathe again. He took several large gulps of fresh air, while at the same time trying to keep them both above the surface of the water.

He turned the girl around so that he could make sure she was alright.

But she wasn't alright. She had gone quiet and limp. Her face was blue, and she wasn't breathing.

Chapter Eleven

Hedge started to panic. What was he supposed to do? He forced himself to think, but it was so hard, the cold water was tortuous and his hands and feet felt had become quite numb. He couldn't remember all the details of resuscitation, so he simply opened the girl's mouth wide and blew several large breaths of air into her windpipe. Next, he squeezed her chest tightly a few times, before blowing more air into her mouth. As he did so she suddenly coughed violently, and a large spurt of seawater shot from her throat.

Emily started screaming. 'Get off me…. Where's my mum…. I'm drowning ….. Help…I'm cold …'

Hedge held her tight and tried to calm her. 'It's alright, Emily, you're safe now. I'm going to look after you. Someone is coming to help us.'

Emily relaxed a little, and he continued to hold her tightly. He was so very tired now, and all the feeling had gone from his legs. Even his head felt cold. He tried to work out how long they had been in the water, maybe fifteen minutes, or twenty, he wasn't sure. The alarm from other passengers on the ship would have been given immediately, and it would take maybe thirty minutes for a rescue boat to arrive to pick them up. Could he hold on to the girl for that long, and keep them both afloat, he didn't think so.

The water seemed to be consuming him. He felt like his body was slipping away. Emily had gone quiet again. They bobbed up and down with the swell of the sea. The cruise liner was no longer in sight. Hedge felt afraid, cold, and very lonely. He tried to keep his eyes open, but he just felt numb.

He was just so incredibly tired and so cold, and terrified.

Still holding onto the young girl, he waited. And he waited. He had to kick his legs to keep them both afloat. It was tiring, and his left foot hurt badly.

More time passed.

Next thing he knew, he was in the middle of a dream, but somehow it also felt real. There was a loud noise, like an engine with a steady beating rhythm. It was very close, and it felt like his eardrums were going to burst. It was windy, like in the middle of a tornado. The force of the wind was pushing him below the waves. It must have been a dream as he couldn't feel anything. His body was still numb. He couldn't focus his eyes, and there were bright lights shining down on him. There was a noise echoing around him, but he couldn't make out what it was. It was like someone shouting through a narrow tunnel.

He tried to make out what the voice was saying. '.... is ...... United ...... Coastguard...... down..... rescue .....'

It didn't make any sense to him. It was all so confusing, the lights, the noise, the cold, the pain, the tiredness - he just wanted it to stop. He closed his eyes and hoped it would all go away.

The winch operator on the Sikorsky MH-60T Jayhawk leaned out from the side door of the helicopter and repeated his message. He was speaking into his helmet microphone which was being relayed to a powerful loudspeaker slung below the body of the helicopter.

'This is the United States Coastguard. We are going to winch down and rescue you. Please raise one arm to show us that you understand what we are saying.'

The winch operator shook his head to no one in particular. He clicked his microphone so that he could talk to the pilot of the Sikorsky. 'Take her lower a few more feet and then I'm going down. I can see both of them, so I'll bring them up together. It looks like they are in a bad way, so have the medics ready.'

He leaned his body out of the aircraft and his assistant operator lowered him down using the on-board winch controls. As he got close to the two bodies in the water, he gave further instructions to the pilot so that he ended up in exactly the right position. He landed in the sea next to Hedge, and quickly clipped a harness around him. He took a firm hold of the girl and signalled for them all to be winched back aboard.

A few moments later all three of them were safely inside the helicopter cabin. The coastguard medics immediately started work on Hedge and Emily. The little girl was whimpering quietly, but Hedge was silent. He lay still, hardly breathing, and his skin was pale and dull.

He no longer felt cold and tired. He no longer felt anything.

Chapter Twelve

It was evening that same day when Hedge stirred from his sleep. He was in a very comfortable bed in a recently refurbished wing of a Puerto Rican hospital. The doctor was just coming round the ward to check on the various patients under his supervision. He noticed that Hedge had woken and so headed over towards him.

'How are you feeling young man?' he said with a broad smile.

'I feel okay, but a bit hungry. What happened to me?'

The doctor leaned over to take a closer look at him. 'You went for a little swim in our sea, don't you remember? Not a clever thing to do really, as it's quite dangerous out there. It may be the Caribbean, but out in the middle of it the temperature can be quite cold. You suffered some hypothermia, but it was only temporary, and you seem to be okay now. I have advised the ship's captain that you are okay to resume your journey, so the coastguard is going to give you a lift back to the boat.'

The events of the day were coming back to Hedge slowly. He asked about the young girl, and the doctor explained that she had already been repatriated with her family on board the cruise ship. Apparently children are less prone to shock and cold than adults, so recovery is often quicker. The doctor suggested that Hedge should get a decent meal inside him and then leave at the earliest opportunity, to avoid delaying the ship further. And also to get away from the local media interest in him, which was growing by the minute.

Hedge sat up and slowly eased himself off the bed. As he put his weight down on his feet he winced as he suddenly remembered his accident with the rear railing on the ship. His foot had been neatly bandaged but it still hurt. A nurse had approached and told him he needed to go careful on it for a few days and report to his local doctor when he returned home.

Hedge dressed in some fresh clothes provided by the nurse, and followed her down to the hospital canteen. He ordered himself some hot coffee and a plate of freshly made pasta. He wolfed this down quickly and then asked the orderly on duty for a large slice of apple pie. He had almost finished this when a coastguard officer appeared at the door of the canteen and beckoned to him. They both headed off towards the elevator and took this to the roof of the hospital, where the helicopter was waiting.

The coastguard was a friendly man called Jim. He told Hedge that they worked alongside the US military, and operated out of a base on the island of Puerto Rico. The two of them chatted through their helmet intercom sets as the aircraft headed out to sea. Jim explained that the ship had carried on with its journey, albeit at a slower pace in order to allow Hedge to catch up with it.

After about forty five minutes they sighted the cruise liner in the distance, and a short while later the helicopter was hovering gently over the front of the ship. There was no helipad on the vessel, so Hedge had to be winched the short distance down onto the deck. Once he was free of the harness, he turned and waved goodbye as the helicopter lifted away and headed back in the direction from which it had come.

Hedge brushed himself down as his clothes had become ruffled. He was wearing a pair of blue denim trousers and a navy blue sweater. He had a coastguard jacket on over the top of this. Clearly they didn't want this back, he thought to himself, so he would keep it as a souvenir.

He turned to see which way he needed to go to get back to his cabin. It was only now that he noticed that what must have been the entire population of the ship had gathered on the various decks at the front of the boat, all looking down at where he stood. There was a massive cheer from the crowd, and the captain stepped forward to greet Hedge with a firm handshake. The captain leaned towards him and said something, but he couldn't hear what it was due to the noise from the gathered crowd.

Hedge looked up at all the people staring down at him. There were hundreds of them, all waving and shouting. It seemed amazing to him that the ship could carry all of these people at the same time. As he continued to cast his eyes around the throng of people, he suddenly spotted Maddie, and he held his hand up to her. She waved back excitedly.

As quickly as it had started, the noise of the crowd began to quieten. Then there was almost complete silence. Hedge didn't immediately understand what had caused this reduction in volume. He looked at the captain, and then turned his head back to the crowd, but still he could see no reason for the change in atmosphere.

Then he saw her. A young girl wearing a pale blue dress was walking towards him, carrying in her hand a small bunch of brightly coloured flowers. Emily was smiling at him. She grabbed hold of his hand and looked up at him with an expression of pure adoration.

The crowd began to cheer once more until the noise became deafening. Hedge looked up and smiled, and as he did so he wiped his eyes with his free hand. They had strangely begun to moisten, probably because of the wind, he thought to himself.

Chapter Thirteen

'Everyone on board thinks you're a hero, as do I, of course.' Maddie beamed across at her brother. She looked very proud.

Hedge and Maddie were sitting in the main restaurant on the cruise ship having just eaten a very pleasant lunch. Maddie was explaining to him that the ship's captain had taken the very unusual step of asking all the passengers to vote on whether he should slow the ship down to wait for you, or let you make your own way back to England. Apparently the boat was almost out of range of the Puerto Rican coastguard service. A German passenger named Muller had complained so bitterly about the slowdown, that the captain had finally settled on letting the passengers all have their say.

The vote had been quickly arranged, with two ballot boxes being passed around the ship. A steward had returned the boxes to the captain later in the day for him to oversee the counting. The 'no' box was opened first to count the votes of those who wished for the ship not to slow down. The captain immediately began shouting at the steward for wasting his time, by accidentally bringing him the wrong box. This one was empty. The steward was to go away and bring back the correct 'no' box. The steward explained that this was the correct box. None of the passengers had voted 'no'. The captain thought that strange as he remembered the German man who was so opposed to the idea. Apparently, the steward explained, that no one had seen Herr Muller all afternoon, except for a cabin steward, who felt sure he had spotted the German with a terrible black eye. His wife, however, had been seen walking alone around the upper viewing deck. She hadn't spoken to anyone, but several of the passengers thought it strange that she had her hands covered with a pair of dark, cotton gloves.

Hedge was listening to the story with interest, but he hadn't yet had the chance to ask Maddie what he was desperate to know. Eventually she finished talking.

'How did you know, about the girl?'

Maddie frowned as she replied. 'As I mentioned to you shortly after we first met, I get this voice in my head occasionally, and it speaks to me. Sometimes what it says doesn't make any sense, but I listen anyway. It happens only now and again, maybe just two or three times a year.'

'I remember you telling me about that, but I thought it didn't happen anymore.'

'It's not very often, only now and again. It's not just a voice though, sometimes I can see what's about to happen. It seems like a movie playing out before my eyes, but it's blurred and indistinct.'

'That's amazing.' Hedge said.

They called over a waiter and ordered some more drinks, along with two banana flavoured muffins. They sat quietly until the waiter returned with their order, genuinely comfortable in each other's company.

'I think you told me before about the incident with the bear and your uncle's friends. Just remind me of that story.'

He could sense Maddie didn't really like talking about it, so he gave her time to see if she would respond. Eventually she started talking again.

'It was a few years ago now, near the beginning of summer. I was walking back from college one afternoon. I was alone, and almost home when the voice spoke to me.'

'Don't let him go.'

'That's all it said, nothing more. I had no idea what it meant, so I ignored it. Then the next morning as I was brushing my teeth, the voice repeated the same words.'

'Don't let him go.'

'It made no sense to me, until my uncle told me at breakfast that his friend Jake was going camping in the mountains with some other guys the following weekend. Was it connected to that? I wasn't sure. So still I ignored the voice. Then on the morning of the planned camping trip, I awoke early, dripping with sweat, like I had some kind of fever. The voice said the same words again.'

'Don't let him go.'

'I quickly got dressed and walked down the road, to where my uncle's friend lived. He had a pickup parked in his driveway, and he was loading it up for the trip. We chatted for a couple of minutes. I always got on well with Jake, he was very easy going. Then suddenly, I just blurted out that he should cancel his trip. He laughed, and said he couldn't and that he had been planning it for ages. I tried to convince him but he just told me to go home and annoy someone else. I didn't have any good reason to convince him not to go, and I certainly couldn't tell him about the voice.'

Hedge was listening intently. 'So what happened?'

'I couldn't think what to do, and then I saw a hunting knife sticking out of the side pocket of a bag in the back of the pickup. I grabbed it and before he could stop me I slashed one of the rear tyres of his vehicle. He was livid, but I just ran off home.'

'So he didn't go then?'

'No. He couldn't get a replacement vehicle, and his friends had already left. They went off without him. When my uncle heard about it later, he stormed into my room in a rage and asked what the hell I thought I was doing. I didn't have an explanation, so he beat me with one of his walking sticks as a punishment.'

Hedge looked horrified. 'I'd like to give him a good hiding someday.'

Maddie ignored this and carried on with the story.

'Anyway, everything changed several days later, when the local news reported that three men had been attacked by a bear whilst sleeping in the forest. The reporter told how one man had died after having his head partially crushed in the animals jaw. Another of the campers had been mauled so badly that surgeons had to later amputate his left arm. The third man escaped relatively unscathed and had managed to raise the alarm. My uncle sat at home and listened to the news about the three men. When the reporter finished, my uncle slowly turned his head towards me. He was deep in thought, and he was shaking his head very slowly from side to side.

He tried to say something to me, but no words came out of his mouth. I just smiled at him. A few minutes later he stood up and went out to the garage, and gathering up all his sticks, he laid them in a heap on the back garden. It took a little while, but eventually he managed to set fire to the bundle with his cigarette lighter.'

'What did he say when he came back indoors?'

'He said nothing. Not that day, or the next. In fact, it has never been mentioned again. That was the last time he ever beat me too, he has never laid a finger on me since then. The only time he ever referred to it, was a few months later when I overheard him tell a neighbour that he thought I was psychotic. He meant psychic of course.'

They chatted together for a little longer and then he headed out on deck for some fresh air. The boat was pushing its way through the sea, heading away from Cuba now. Hedge had missed the ship docking there while he was laid up in hospital. He was disappointed, as he wanted to see the old town of Havana.

'I'll probably never see it now,' he mumbled to himself.

If only he knew then how wrong he was.

Chapter Fourteen

Cole was watching the three men very carefully.

It was obvious to him that they were professionals. He could spot a trained killer from a long way off. Was it that certain hard look on their faces, mixed in with their slow, confident movements? Or, more likely, it was that innate ability that these kinds of people had to look completely relaxed, whilst at the same time being in a state of permanent alert.

Not including himself and the Irish guys he was tailing, he counted another nine people in the bar that afternoon. Although the three men hid them well, to Cole it was obvious that they were all carrying handguns. No one else in the bar would have known that. Neither would they have known who he was currently working for.

Cole hated being involved in MI5 operations. He didn't have a regular job as such, not since he had left the British army. Because of his Special Forces training though, a few years back he had been recommended to the then Prime Minister for a particular task. He had done well, and since that time he had carried out a few small but unpleasant jobs directly for the British government.

He took another long gulp from his pint of Guinness. He wasn't a great fan of that particular brew, but as he was drinking in an Irish pub he hadn't wanted to draw undue attention to himself. As he placed his glass back down on the counter, he caught sight of his reflection in the large mirror behind the bar. He looked old for his forty something years. The dark brown hair he deliberately kept short was now starting to show some signs of greying. His face was well tanned, due to the travelling he often did to remote, mainly warm, destinations.

'How come all the bad stuff seems to happen in hot countries?' He mumbled to himself. He couldn't remember ever being sent to Canada or Greenland to sort out any warring factions. Okay, there's always Russia he thought. Quite a lot of that is bloody freezing.

His thinking was interrupted when one of the Irishmen moved away from the pool table, and headed in the direction of the men's toilet. Cole decided to follow him. As it happened, he was desperate for a piss himself. The brief he had been given for this task was just to keep an eye on the three men, and any other suspicious activity occurring in the bar. It was especially important to look out for known Irish terrorist suspects, and sympathisers. The actions of such groups had diminished rapidly in recent years, mainly as a result of the peace agreements. But there was still some level of threat posed by such people.

Initially Cole had told his current employer to 'go screw themselves.' He didn't like working for MI5, or any of the British spy agencies, preferring instead to operate directly through government ministers. There may not be an 'I' in 'Team' as corporate bosses often like to espouse, but, as he said on one occasion to the deputy head of MI6, in response to the same phrase, 'there is an "O" in "Fuck off."'

In this instance though, the pay on offer had been good. The contract was only for four weeks, and he needed the money.

He weaved his way down to the back of the pub, and pushed open the door to the toilet. Inside the smell was horrific. Stale piss had a lingering odour, and it was clear that these toilets didn't get a regular daily clean.

The first urinal was occupied and so Cole moved past it casually. Turning to face him, the tall, gaunt-looking man smiled as he spoke.

'Hi there, not a bad place this don't you think. Do you drink here regularly?'

Cole was pretty good with Irish accents. He had spent several years in Belfast. This guy was almost certainly from Londonderry, or Derry, whichever you prefer.

'Not regularly, just now and again.' Cole fumbled with the zipper on his jeans. Like most men, he found it slightly unnerving to have a conversation with a complete stranger when you are both standing side by side trying to piss.

The gaunt faced man stared straight ahead at the wall in front of him as he said his next sentence.

'Are you SAS or MI5?'

'Neither.' Cole replied without hesitation. Technically it was true of course. He had in the past served in the Special Air Service for six years, and he was on a job for MI5 at the present time, but not directly employed by that organisation.

'You think I don't know a Watcher when I see one.' The man laughed. 'You're good, but not as good as you believe you are.'

'Just trying to enjoy a pint and a piss, that's all.' Cole had started to wash his hands. He straightened up from the washbasin when he felt the jab in his lower back.

Cole fought the urge to turn around. 'I hope you know how to use that shooter. If not, I'm going to take it from you and ram it up your arse.'

'It's SAS then, judging from the bad attitude.' The Irishman pushed Cole towards the toilet door. 'Turn right when we get back into the hallway, then out the back door into the rear courtyard. It's quiet there. You and I are going to have some fun.'

'You haven't washed your hands yet? If you want to touch my dick, then you'd better be clean before you do so.'

The Irishman didn't answer. He pushed Cole towards the back door, opened it, and then shoved him into the cool air outside. This guy won't be so confident once he and his two mates had finished with him, he thought to himself.

Chapter Fifteen

The small enclosed area at the back of the pub was deserted, apart from the three Irishmen and Cole. In warmer weather drinkers would often sit at one of the wooden tables scattered randomly around. But today the air was cool, and rain was threatening.

The man who Cole had met in the toilet was still holding the handgun. Cole knew his weapons. This was a standard Glock 17. German made, efficient and reliable.

The other two Irishmen stood close by. Like the first one, they looked fit, tough, and alert.

Cole sounded remarkably confident when he spoke. 'As you'll appreciate, things don't look good for you three guys. The odds are stacked against you. Sure, you look tough enough, and you've got weapons. But as your friend here rightly guessed, I have been trained by British Special Forces. So, let's do this the easy way. Firstly, hand over your guns to me. Then you can tell me what you're up to. And after that, I'll call Scotland Yard who will send a van to give you a ride in. How does that sound?'

'That seems like a reasonable offer to me.' The man holding the Glock replied with a serious expression. 'What do you think boys?'

The man nearest to Cole responded first. With lightning speed, he pulled a small, leather cosh from his jacket pocket, took a pace closer to Cole and hit him on the left arm with all the force he could muster.

Cole shouted out. It had hurt. Worse than that, he was sure he felt a bone break somewhere in his lower arm. Now the other guy had joined in. He must have been holding a heavy ball bearing, or something similar, in his fist, as when his bunched right hand landed on Cole's face, once more he felt the sound of a breaking bone.

Cole's head was spinning. He hadn't even had time to fight back, as blow after blow landed on him. Then he was on the floor. Heavily booted feet were kicking him from all angles. A sharp pain welled up from one of his kidneys as a steel toecap found its target. He could taste blood in his mouth, and he felt sure he had swallowed one of his own teeth.

The man holding the gun knelt down on Cole's chest. The weight on top of him meant he could hardly breathe.

'Is it even worth me asking who you are and why you are watching us? Would it save time if I assume you would die before you told me anything?'

Cole lifted his head up a fraction. It took all his effort to do so. At first when he tried to speak, no sound came out as his throat was sticky with his own congealed blood. Then he coughed and managed to clear a small area around his vocal chords.

'Good assumption, you dickhead,' Cole spluttered.

Then he passed out.

He awoke some time later. His body was still screaming with pain from its various fractures and bruises. It took a while, but eventually Cole managed to focus his eyes. He was still outside, but in a different location. They had obviously moved him while he was unconscious. He appeared to be near to some kind of industrial estate. There were several small warehouses and workshops close by. The three men had tied him securely to a steel framed chair, and this was resting on a concrete pathway. The path ran alongside a river, or possibly a canal, and a gentle current was flowing.

'This is your last chance to tell me why you are following us.' The gaunt-looking man had put his gun away. He checked up and down the river path to make sure there was no one else around. The place was deserted.

'And if I do, you'll let me go?'

'Yes, of course.'

'Okay, I'll talk.' Cole looked resigned. The Irishman smiled, and then he kneeled down expectantly in front of the chair to listen to what his prisoner had to say. It was unusual for Special Forces men to break, but not entirely unknown. When faced with imminent death, people will do the most unpredictable things.

Cole coughed to clear his throat. He moved to wipe one of his hands across his mouth, but then remembered that both of them were securely tied to the chair. He straightened himself up as he spoke.

'I followed the three of you into the bar just before midday. You looked like the men I was told to keep a watch on. They gave me photos.'

'So why were they interested in us?'

'Well, Scotland Yard have some updated anti-terrorist laws in place, and they're looking to make some early arrests under Section 418 of the new regulations. You guys fitted the bill perfectly.'

The Irishman frowned. '418, what's that about?'

Cole hesitated for a couple of seconds before he replied. 'Anyone with a dick less than half an inch long is to be immediately detained. You three boys are under arrest.'

The gaunt man scowled, stood up straight, and then kicked the steel chair backwards into the water. Cole was still laughing when he hit the river, although he did manage to take a large lungful of air just before he submerged beneath the surface of the water.

Chapter Sixteen

The water was cold, but not particularly deep.

As he landed on the river bed, the old saying about how you can drown in just two inches of water came rushing into his head.

Cole was not in two inches of water though. The river was around four feet deep. But the chair had landed on its back, and his hands and feet were securely tied to the steel tubes that made up the chair. As he hit the water, he had taken in a decent gulp of fresh air, and he estimated that he had around one minute's oxygen in his lungs.

He tried to roll the chair over. Perhaps if he did so then he could try and stand up. It was hopeless though. His arms still ached from the recent beating he'd been given, and he had very little strength left. Many years ago, during scuba training, he had learnt that letting out very small amounts of air slowly actually extended the amount of breathing time you had overall. So gently, he bubbled air out of his mouth. He sensed it helped, but not much.

Thirty seconds had already passed and he was now starting to panic. Again he tried to move the chair, with no luck. He could feel the cold current passing slowly over him. With all the power he could muster, he pulled at the bonds holding his arms. A piercing pain ran down his arm as he did so. He remembered the sound of bone breaking when the cosh had landed.

His vision was blurred by the cloudy water, but he noticed that the figures watching him from above the water suddenly turned around and moved quickly away. Then he heard some shouting noises, and then nothing.

It must have been a full minute since he had entered the water, and his lungs were bursting. He was desperate now. There had been many life-threatening situations over the years, and he knew it would end like this one day. But he didn't want it to be today. He breathed out the last of his air. His lungs were screaming at him. He tried desperately to override the automatic breathing reflex that the human body has. But it was impossible. He had to draw breath. No matter how hard he tried to, he couldn't hold back.

He sucked a huge gulp of river water straight down into his lungs. Then, for the second time that day, he started to black out.

Many sensations came at him all at once. He was being lifted, then the terrible coughing that wouldn't end. Next, the loud voice shouting at him to keep still, and the horrendous pressure on his chest. It felt like his ribs were about to crack. Now he was being sick. He swallowed some of it and it tasted vile. And there was the laughter, always that buoyant laughter.

There was a thin man, in a well-cut, black suit. He was holding out his hand flat, palm upwards, towards the guy next to him. This other man was taller, bulkier, and he had a long, brown beard. He was wearing a similar suit to his colleague, and identical dark sunglasses.

'That's the easiest fifty pounds I'll make this month. I knew he would last more than a minute. You should have more faith.' The thin man was smiling as he collected his winnings.

'I didn't think he took much air in before he went down. I'm sure he wasn't going to survive that ducking.' The taller man seemed dejected.

Cole had almost regained his normal breathing pattern. He was still in shock, and felt terrible. But at least he was alive. He nodded towards the suited men.

'MI5?'

'Indeed.' The thin one replied. 'Just keeping an eye on you, that's all.'

'Where are those three Irish bastards?'

'Probably back in the pub. I don't think they'd quite finished their game of pool.' The MI5 man seemed fairly casual about the whole situation.

Cole was incensed. 'Go and pick them up. I want those fuckers in custody.'

The man shrugged. 'I hardly think so. We don't arrest suspected top level terrorists just for pushing someone into a river. Better to wait for something much bigger dear boy. Anyway, get yourself cleaned up. We have an appointment in thirty minutes.'

'And who would that be with?'

'The Home Secretary, it seems he wants you to go on a little trip for him.'

Chapter Seventeen

The thin-looking agent in the smart, black suit had introduced himself to Cole as Simpson. He hadn't mentioned anything about a first name. Apart from that, they said very little else to each other on the way to the meeting with the Home Secretary.

Cole was still feeling irritated. Not so much from the fact that he had almost drowned, it annoyed him more knowing that his survival had been the subject of a small wager.

The car they were travelling in had heavily tinted windows, so it wasn't easy to see exactly where they were going. The driver expertly weaved his way between the central London traffic. Eventually they stopped outside a smart looking Italian restaurant, and they were both shown through to a private function room.

Once inside, they sat at a small table. Cole immediately recognised the Home Secretary, Alistair Brown. He seemed younger than the pictures of him that were shown regularly on television news articles. But he was friendly and very polite, and they chatted together for a few minutes, exchanging pleasantries mainly on the subject of family.

Brown broke off the conversation for a couple of minutes while he finished the rest of his meal. It looked like he was eating ravioli, as on his plate was a small heap of pasta parcels, covered in a rich, tomato sauce. Eventually he laid his fork neatly on the plate, pushed the remaining garlic bread to one side, and carefully wiped his mouth with a white serviette.

He turned his focus back towards Cole and started to explain why he had asked to see him.

'It seems we have a difficult situation on our hands. And you, Mr. Cole, have a reputation for helping us to sort out these kinds of things.'

'What kind of thing are we talking about?' Cole tried to sound respectful, but at the same time he was beginning to worry about what the man meant by 'a difficult situation'.

'I'm going to be quite frank with you. My honourable friend, the Education Minister, has in the past engaged in some extracurricular activities.'

'Some extra what?' Cole was shaking his head.

'In layman's terms, he was shagging an impressionable young lady member of his team. To cut a long story short, a while later she gave birth to a daughter, and the Minister agreed to financially support the child. He felt it was his duty to do so. And he certainly didn't want any adverse publicity. The only condition being that the young lady and her new daughter leave England.'

Cole smiled. 'So all's well in the world then?'

'Not quite.' Brown continued the story. 'All was well until recently. Mother and daughter were enjoying their new life in the United States. But the daughter has gone missing, as of last week. The FBI believes that she may have been kidnapped, possibly as part of an international child smuggling ring. But they have no firm evidence to back that up. The mother is distraught, and is demanding that the British authorities provide some help. She is desperate to find her daughter.'

Cole wasn't smiling any more. 'So your government friend wants to help. Otherwise he may end up with some of that bad publicity he was so desperately hoping to avoid.'

Brown nodded. 'You have grasped the situation nicely.'

'And you want me to get involved. That way it doesn't look like the British authorities are interfering.'

Brown nodded again.

'And so I'm on my own. I'll have no back-up, no authority, and ...' Cole hesitated just a second '... I'll be totally expendable.'

The Home Secretary looked slightly shocked. He raised his right hand and wagged his index finger back and forth, in a manner that refuted Cole's accusation.

'That's not entirely true. Well, most of it is, but of course you won't be on your own. I've been looking back over your history, at some of the important tasks that you have so successfully carried out for the government in the past. We think we have the ideal person to support you in this operation, and he is already in the region.'

'What region would that be?'

Brown picked up a sheet of paper and briefly glanced at it.

'According to my intelligence report, the man I am thinking of is on a ship very close to Cuba. And by all accounts, he is being treated as a bit of a hero by the local press. I understand that he is a good friend of yours.'

Cole had no idea who he could be talking about.

Chapter Eighteen

Hedge hadn't expected all the fuss that now surrounded him. It turned out that the young girl's grandfather was of Cuban origin. The newspapers in that country had picked up on the story, and Hedge was now being treated like a minor celebrity on board the ship.

The Caribbean trip though was coming to an end, and soon Hedge and his sister would be on their way back to England.

It was the last day of the cruise, and Hedge found himself idling the time away on the top deck of the ship. He had found a quiet spot and settled back in a very comfortable deckchair. As he lay there, he began thinking about his life, as he often did. He hadn't always lived in England. In fact, he was born in the United States. His family originally came from near Houston, in Texas, so he was officially an American citizen. His father had been in the US Air Force, and the family had moved to England when he was just eight years old. His dad had been part of the 48th Fighter Wing, otherwise known as the Statue of Liberty Wing, which was based at Lakenheath in Suffolk, a very pleasant part of England.

Tragically, just after Hedge had celebrated his tenth birthday, both his parents had been killed in a car crash near the base.

At the time he had no brothers or sisters, so he had felt quite alone in the world. His uncle Larry had taken charge of the funeral and other formalities, and Hedge had then gone to live with him and his family in London. They had two of their own children, a boy and a girl, and they had all been happy to welcome him into their home. His uncle was employed in a senior position with a large bank, and Hedge had found his work at the bank of great interest.

Despite the trauma of losing his parents, he had done reasonably well for himself. His Uncle had paid for him to go to a good English boarding school, and following that he had attended Cambridge University. He wasn't what might be described as a top student, but he had worked hard, and had done just enough to scrape his place at one of England's finest places of learning.

He had enjoyed his time in Cambridge, but he had been keen to get out into the wider world and start his career. With a little help from his uncle Larry, he had secured a position in a small investment bank in London. He had lost that job though, after spending a short time in prison. He had been found guilty of 'insider trading', although he hadn't intentionally set out to do anything wrong.

Hedge kept himself in good shape due to regular visits to a local gym. He was a fraction under six feet tall, with dark hair, and, as he was often told, he had a very pale complexion.

Although everyone called him Hedge, that wasn't actually his real name. His passport stated him as Tom Millar. The only person who still called him Tom though, was his aunt. To everyone else he was simply known as Hedge. The reason for this was that for as long as anyone could remember, he had been fascinated with money and finance. Even as a young boy he would keep a record of his pocket money. When he was at junior school in Houston, he had regularly followed the share price movements on the New York stock exchange. He read financial magazines and books, and he had been a daily reader of the Financial Times ever since he had moved into his uncle's house in London.

When he was just seven years old, before the family had moved to England, his father had asked him what he wanted to be when he grew up. To everyone's amazement he had announced that he would like to be a 'Hedge Fund Manager'. He wasn't actually sure what one of those was at the time, but he knew it was an important financial job, and anyway, he quite liked the sound of it.

So the name had stuck, and from then on everyone had called him Hedge. Most people who knew him now would probably not even be aware of his real name.

His thoughts came back to the present as one of the ships stewards was scurrying towards him. There were no other passengers in the immediate vicinity, so Hedge assumed the man wanted to speak to him.

'Excuse me but are you Mr. Millar.'

'Yes, that's me. Is there a problem?'

'No sir, I hope not. I have a message for you though. It's been sent through on the ship's radio, which is rather unusual.'

Hedge took the piece of notepaper he was offered. He opened it cautiously and started to read.'

'Hello old mate. I hope you're keeping well. I have good news. The old team is back again. You and I are now on assignment on behalf of Her Majesty's government. I'll meet you in Havana in two days time in the bar of the Imperial Hotel at midday local time. No need to bring cash or weapons, I'll sort all that. See you soon. Regards, Cole.'

Hedge folded the note and stuffed it into his bag. Then he took a deep breath.

'Shit, fuck, and shit,' he said to no one in particular.

The steward looked shocked. 'Oh dear, it sounds quite bad.'

Hedge looked towards the man, whose face had turned quite pale.

'No, it's not,' he said as he shook his head.

'It's much worse than that.'

Chapter Nineteen

The cargo plane touched down at Luqa airport just after midnight local time. All aircraft arriving in Malta would land here as it's the only airport on the island. It was a dark night as, unusually, the entire sky was covered with a thick layer of cloud, preventing the moonlight from casting its glow. The pilot had made the journey from Cuba many times before and this was the aircraft's normal refuelling stop. He taxied close to one of the service hangers as directed by the ground staff. As soon as he was given the okay, he shut down the four turboprop engines and waited for the fuel tanker to arrive.

The aircraft was very distinctive, an Antonov An-12, built in Russia in the early 1970's. Originally used by the military, many had now found their way into private hands either as collector's items, or still in operation flying cargo around the world. The range of the standard version of the An-12 is less than six thousand kilometres, but this particular plane had been upgraded to carry more fuel. It could therefore cope with the nine thousand kilometre journey it had just made from Havana.

Refuelling stops were bad news. They attracted unwanted attention.

Pablo unlocked the side door of the plane and rolled out the metal step ladder. Like the pilot, he was familiar with this particular journey, and knew the routine. It normally took the local customs inspector at least thirty minutes to arrive, but it had been known to take much longer. On their previous stopover the guy hadn't come to see them until they had been on the ground for almost two hours.

Tonight though, he was prompt. But as the inspector climbed the steps up to the cargo area, Pablo knew straight away that he had a huge problem on his hands.

'Hi, so where is Mr. Vella, the usual customs officer?'

The man was breathing heavily after the exertion of the steps. He was clearly unfit. 'It appears we have a fever going around the office, and another person has just gone home early feeling very unwell. It's good that we are not busy tonight.'

'That's too bad about Vella. I hope he gets well soon. Hopefully we won't keep you too long here. My name is Pablo. I'm the cargo manager on board.' He held out his hand as a friendly gesture, but his voice couldn't disguise his nervousness.

'My name is Borg, and I will be as long as I need to be. Even if we are short on staff, that's no reason not to be thorough. And it's no good trying to bribe me with any of those expensive Cuban cigars you have on board, that simply won't work.'

As soon as he'd said this, Borg let out a huge belly laugh. He clearly found his own humour highly entertaining, and it was some time before he managed to stop his chortling. Eventually, he pulled out a plain, white handkerchief from his shirt pocket and carefully wiped the sweat from his forehead. The man had a balding head, with just a few thin wisps of brown hair remaining. His face was round, and it sat upon an unusually short neck. From his demeanour so far, he appeared to have two extremes of behaviour, either total hilarity or utter seriousness.

It was the latter which he had now reverted to. 'I need to see your certified manifest. Please fetch me a copy.'

His eyes scanned up and down the cargo deck. It was only then that he noticed the other person. 'Who is that?'

The woman he was staring at was sitting on a seat provided for the aircrew. She had short-cropped, blonde hair, and her face was pale and striking. Not what would be classed as especially attractive, but the hard lines of her jaw and cheekbones gave her a definite eastern European look.

'That's Olga. Our company's Middle-East Liaison Manager. She's hitching a ride to Jordan with us. I think the idea is that she can establish new contacts there for our goods.'

Borg looked mystified. 'So your boss is a comedian?'

'What do you mean?' Pablo frowned. He was still nervous. This guy Borg worried him.

'So, your company sends a woman to deal with Arab customers. That should go down well.'

The sarcasm wasn't lost on Pablo. He shrugged his shoulders in response, but said nothing.

The serious look had returned to Borg's face. 'How many people do you have on board?'

'There's just Olga, myself, and the two pilots.' Pablo swallowed hard as he gave his reply. He hoped that the customs official hadn't noticed his nervous response.

'I need to see passports for all those personnel. And that manifest. Let's get on with this.'

Pablo turned and hurried off to find the documents. This was not how things normally worked. What the hell was he going to do with the five thousand US dollars he had brought along from Havana? Clearly this Borg guy was not expecting the cash. He genuinely seemed to want to inspect the list of goods on board. Had Vella not explained the process to him? Obviously he hadn't.

'Shit. What do we do now?' Pablo mumbled to himself. 'Shit. Shit.'

Chapter Twenty

Borg inspected the four passports he'd been given by Pablo. They all seemed in order. The three men on the flight were Cuban nationals, but it was the woman's document that he spent the most time looking at.

'So you are Estonian. What part of that country are you from?'

Olga raised herself from her seat and approached the Maltese official. She was tall and lean, he noticed. Her black jeans were skin tight, and perfectly complimented the baggy, white cotton top she was wearing.

'I was born in the capital, Tallinn.'

'It's a beautiful city. My wife and I visited a few years ago. The town centre is magical. It reminded us of a scene from an old fairy tale. What's the name of the lovely square in the heart of the old town? The one with the beautiful little church and the small cafes dotted around.'

'I wouldn't know,' said Olga. Her tone was a little terse. Some would say rude, but that would be to misunderstand the natural abruptness of the inhabitants of the Baltic States.

Borg held up her passport. 'But you are from Estonia, are you not?'

'Born there yes, but we moved to Latvia when I was very young. I don't remember anything about my home country.'

'Whatever, they are all basically the same country, all of them Russian at the end of the day.'

'Not Russian.' Olga's eyes flashed wildly as she spat out her words.

Borg nodded. Clearly he had touched a nerve. There was something about this woman, pleasant exterior, but hard inside. His serious expression was still present as he handed the passports back to Pablo. 'Pass me the manifest please. Let's sample some of this shall we?'

'There's really no need. The entire cargo is made up of fresh fruit, tobacco products, and various kinds of seeds.'

'And that needs to be delivered by plane? Could it not be transported by sea?' Borg had started to sense some nervousness in these two. The man called Pablo had been worried ever since he had boarded the plane. He could tell that. It was all part of the training. But now the woman too, she concerned him. Something about her wasn't right.

Borg held out his hand. 'The manifest if you please.'

The three of them walked down the body of the aircraft. A standard An-12 would normally be able to carry around twenty metric tonnes of payload. This aircraft was well short of that. The biggest single product line aboard was only three tons of speciality cigars, all manufactured by hand in Havana. The story goes that the tobacco leaves are rolled on the thighs of young, attractive women. This particular brand was indeed hand rolled, but none of the product had been anywhere near any young ladies legs.

Borg stopped walking. He turned and banged his hand against a wooden crate. 'Open this one please.'

'It's just bags of seeds. Look, it's marked clearly on the side.' Pablo pointed to where the crate had been stamped with the words 'Melon Seeds – For Export.'

'Open it.'

The Cuban sighed, stepped forward, and with a small, steel crowbar, he gently prized the lid off the wooden box. He then moved back and, with a wave of his hand, he motioned the customs man forward. The crate was full to the top with clear, plastic bags. Borg picked one up, inspected it, and looking quite satisfied he placed it back on top of the other bags.

The next crate he selected for inspection was full of boxed cigars. Picking up one of the boxes, he made a play of smelling it. Then he turned to Pablo.

'These are good quality, yes?'

Pablo nodded. 'They are some of the best from my island. That package you hold in your hands is worth more than three thousand US dollars.'

'That's a lot of money.'

'It sure is.' Pablo was desperately trying to weigh up the man in front of him.

'Something this valuable would make a good gift for someone.'

'It might.'

'Even a bribe?'

Pablo nodded slowly. He felt sure he could hear his own heart beating.

The official stared at him for a few seconds, and then he gently placed the box of cigars back in the crate.

'Any attempt to influence an officer of a Maltese government department would be a serious crime. If such a thing had happened here today, this aircraft would have been impounded and all personnel aboard would have been immediately detained.'

The man's face became even graver looking. He paced off further along the cargo hold, stopping next to another wooden crate. This one was a slightly different size to the others, and there was only one like it.

'Open this.'

'Surely we have done enough now? All our cargo is as listed on the manifest. We are wasting time. Please, let us carry on with our journey. We have a schedule to meet.' Pablo stopped himself suddenly, realising that he was starting to sound hysterical.

Borg eyed him suspiciously. 'Open this one.'

Pablo stepped towards him, raising the crowbar as he did so. Borg saw the menace in the Cuban's eyes and moved backwards a single pace. He watched in confusion as Pablo slowly placed the crowbar on the crate. He was half expecting a strike from it. He had seen the anger in the man's face. He had seen something else too, fear and desperation, like a wild animal.

But there had been no strike, and no pain. The metal bar had made no contact with him. That didn't make any sense. Why was he feeling dizzy? He was losing consciousness fast. But there had been no heavy blow, no contact.

He was confused.

Then Borg fell forwards and hit the floor of the aircraft hard.

Just before he collapsed he saw the woman, Olga.

She was smiling down at him. And in her right hand he saw a syringe, and it had a needle protruding from the end.

It didn't make any sense.

Chapter Twenty One

The chemical that was now rushing around Borg's body was a variant of a substance known as Suxamethonium Chloride. Similar chemicals are used as general anaesthetics in hospitals. Effectively, once it finds its way into the blood stream it will paralyze the victim for a short period of time. Generally there are few side effects. All that happens is that the person is rendered helpless. Their muscles will simply not respond to any requests for bodily movement from the brain.

Borg found himself feeling very strange. He had landed face up on the floor of the cargo area, and he could still see the man and the woman quite clearly. Bizarrely, he could even hear what they were saying.

'Move him over to the side here.' Pablo had taken hold of the man's shoulders and was hauling him away from the crate he had asked to inspect just a few moments ago. 'What the hell are we going to do with him now?'

'Not that it's for me to tell you how to do your job, but we do need to get this aircraft moving.' Olga had a hint of a smile on her face. She seemed to be enjoying the situation.

Pablo settled the limp body onto a wooden pallet. He looked down at the Maltese official. 'And what do we do with him?'

'We'll worry about that once we are out of here.'

'What, you mean to take him with us?'

'What else do you suggest?' She flashed Pablo a look of astonishment. 'Perhaps we could leave him on the runway here?'

Pablo shook his head. 'Not a good idea, I guess.'

He leaned down and searched through the man's jacket pockets. He quickly found what he was looking for. Holding up the official document for Olga to see, he smiled towards her. 'This is just what we need.'

'What is it?'

'It's our customs approval. The lazy bastard has even stamped it already to save him a journey back to his desk. All I need to do is take this over to the airport manager's office, and we can get our take off clearance.'

Olga winked at him. 'You're a clever boy.'

Pablo blushed slightly. The woman had a certain presence, and dressed as she was, he thought she looked very attractive. He glanced down at Borg, still lying motionless on the crate. The man looked a little frightening. His face was still set with his usual serious look, and his eyes were wide open.

'He looks weird,' said Pablo.

The woman laughed. 'He's just excited, that's all. The guy is looking forward to his trip in the big airplane.'

Borg looked up at her. It was strange, but he could clearly hear their conversation. His brain was telling him that he was desperately trying to get up off the floor, but his body wasn't responding in any way. With all his will power he tried to grab hold of the edge of the pallet underneath him, but his fingers just wouldn't respond. It was infuriating.

Now he was screaming at the top of his voice. 'Help me up. I am a government official, and you are both in serious trouble. You must not let this aircraft depart. It is not authorised. Help me up immediately.'

He could hear his voice in his head. The tone was sharp, and the volume was loud. There was extreme anger in what he was saying. But there was a problem. The two people next to him weren't responding to his shouts. Why couldn't they hear him?

What he didn't realise was that the vocal chords in his throat weren't functioning. Also his lips weren't moving, and there was no sound coming from his mouth. Although he could see and hear, the effects of the chemical injection had rendered him completely incapacitated.

Pablo walked across to the wooden crate that Borg had wanted to inspect. He took a key from his pocket. On top of the crate was a locked, wooden flap, about two feet wide and eighteen inches deep. The lock had a black coloured tag on it, which matched the colour of the tag on the key now in his hand. Pablo pushed the key into the locking mechanism. The padlock clicked open. And he then slowly lifted the wooden flap off the crate.

Olga had moved towards the box, and now she leaned over and peered inside. It was dark in there, but some of the light from the cargo area helped to illuminate inside the crate. She drew her head back slightly as a smell of stale air came rushing out at her. Then she leaned back in closer. In front of her was an opening with metal bars clearly visible. Looking further inside, she could make out the small body of the girl. She looked young, no more than six or seven years old. Some of her curly hair was still visible, but other parts of it had stuck to her head, probably as a result of sweating. It was hot inside the box.

'Is everything okay in there?' Pablo had resisted looking himself. He wasn't particularly squeamish. He just didn't like the smell.

'All okay. She looks fine. But we do need to get going.'

'I'll go and get this sorted then.' Pablo held up the customs document. 'I should be back in a few minutes.'

He smiled down at Borg as he passed by.

The Maltese man screamed abuse at him as he left. He tried to grab hold of Pablo's leg to prevent him from leaving.

But, there was no voice, and no arm movement.

Chapter Twenty Two

Pablo was back on board the An-12 within ten minutes. After making his way forward to the cockpit, he advised the chief pilot that they should get clearance for takeoff from the tower shortly.

Back in the cargo area, Olga had been busy. She had completely undressed their captive, and was in the process of shoving all his clothes into a black, plastic bag.

'What are you doing?' Pablo wasn't sure that this was completely necessary. The man lying in front of him was now totally naked. He seemed older without his clothes on somehow. It was the paunch of his belly and the wrinkled skin of his body, which clearly indicated that this was a person who didn't enjoy regular exercise.

'Well, think about it. We need to get rid of the body. When we do so, we don't want anyone to find anything that can link him back to here, or to us.'

Pablo nodded. That sounded reasonable.

Borg, still utterly paralysed, was listening to their conversation. What did she mean 'get rid of the body.' They were talking as if he was no longer alive. He was, very much so. As soon as the injection had worn off, he would be arresting them both for assaulting a Maltese government officer.

Olga had completed the job of bagging up the man's clothes. She moved back towards him and sat down next to Borg.

'How long do you think he will be out for?' Pablo asked.

'Maybe around an hour or so, after that it starts to wear off.'

'Hey, don't do that, he'll enjoy it too much.' Pablo had started to laugh.

His eyes were fixed on Olga's hands. She had taken hold of the man's limp penis and was trying to massage it into life. There was no response though. It was obvious that Borg was still under the influence of the chemical injection.

'I don't think he fancies me.' She laughed.

'He's an idiot if he doesn't,' Pablo blurted out.

Olga turned to face him. 'That's nice of you to say so.'

The Cuban was kneeling next to her. Directly in front of the inert body of Borg. 'Well I mean... It's just that ...' He was blushing slightly, and he couldn't quite find the right words.

Olga had stood up and was now standing behind him. She leaned down and ran her tongue around his ear. As she did so she whispered to him. 'So you think I'm attractive do you.'

Pablo looked around. The woman was smiling. Clearly she was toying with him. Feeling her tongue on his ear lobe had been very exciting. As she had whispered to him, he could sense her hot breath. He had become aroused. The front of his trousers had started to bulge outwards.

This hadn't gone unnoticed. Olga quickly ran her right hand down his shirt and then further until it was inside his underwear. She took hold of his stiff cock and squeezed hard.

'Oh my god, you're so excited.'

Pablo didn't reply. He couldn't. His breathing had quickened sharply, and his eyes had become unfocused. The woman had pulled open the front of his trousers and his erection was sticking out. Her right hand was wrapped tightly around it. She was squeezing it hard, and running her fingers up and down. It was intoxicating for him. He could still feel her warm breath around his ears, and she was pushing her breasts into his back as she held him.

The pace of her stroking had started to quicken, and the grip around his cock was now like a vice. He started to moan gently as he felt his climax approaching. There was a sudden noise as the roar of the Antolov's engines opened up. The woman was telling him to hold on to something as the plane was now taking off. He leant forward and braced himself against a side panel, but all he could think about was the furious pace of Olga's hand on his penis.

Then everything seemed to happen at once. The plane lurched forwards, now released from its braking systems, and it started to hurtle down the runaway. The woman leaning over Pablo could sense he was close, and she bent forwards and bit his ear hard with her teeth. He couldn't hold himself any longer. Both of the woman's hands were firmly around his cock now, stroking him furiously. With a loud gasp, he finally ejaculated, and a long spurt of his come landed across Borg's chest.

Olga stood up and laughed. 'Well at least we haven't made a mess on the floor.'

Pablo was still leaning against the side of the plane. He couldn't believe what had just happened. It had been so erotic. Something he had never expected. In between trying to get his breath back, he was smiling.

Borg was not happy. In fact, he was outraged. He had just witnessed a scene of utter depravity, and to make things completely unbearable, he was now covered in another man's semen. It was disgusting. He tried to move his hands across to wipe his chest, but still they would not react to his commands. He attempted to shout out, but once again there was no sound. He felt like he was going to explode, as he was so mad with rage. As soon as he had recovered from this ordeal he would ensure that these two would go to prison for a very long time. He would make that a personal goal. No one was going to treat him like this.

The noise of the turboprop engines was deafening as the aircraft lifted into the sky. Borg started to wonder what was going to happen next, and he was listened intently to the woman. She had started talking again.

'Now we need to get rid of this idiot. As soon as we are far out to sea, we can chuck him out. I doubt if he'll ever be found. In fact, if we are high enough, his body will disintegrate when it hits the surface of the water.'

Pablo was laughing. Not only was this woman amazingly desirable, but she was also utterly ruthless. He found the mixture of these two things incredibly exciting.

Pablo turned and walked away from the Maltese official. He was still chuckling to himself.

Borg lay on the crate, still completely helpless. He suddenly felt like he wanted to cry.

But he couldn't. His body wouldn't respond.

Chapter Twenty Three

'Look at this. It's perfect.'

Pablo was excited, almost like a schoolboy might be. He had found a hatch in the floor of the cargo area. When opened, it revealed a chute that went down about three metres and then exited the aircraft just behind the rear landing wheel. Fortunately the aircraft wasn't planning to fly at a high altitude. He had already checked with the chief pilot, and opening the hatch for a while shouldn't cause any issue with the plane.

Olga looked down the chute. All she could see was a short tunnel with another hatch over the far end. 'There's another cover at the bottom.'

'Yes, but it has a pressure switch on it. If you push against it, then it will open, briefly at least. Then it shuts automatically again, making a good seal against the outside air. That's why there's not too much noise at the moment.'

'That's clever. What's it for?'

'I guess the Russian military used it as a quick drop off facility for important items. I'm not too sure really.'

'Okay, drag him over here and we'll get rid of him,' Olga said. He's started to freak me out a little anyway. I'm sure his eyes keep following me about. If I didn't know better, you would think he's listening to us.'

They hauled the inert figure of the Maltese customs official over near to the hatch. The opening was only around two feet in diameter, but the body of the man would easily slide down it.

The aircraft had been flying for around fifty minutes. At its average cruising speed of around six hundred kilometres an hour, it would take them almost four hours to reach their ultimate destination, Amman in the kingdom of Jordan. Right now they would be far out in the Mediterranean Sea, possibly somewhere south of the island of Crete.

Pablo had found a length of braided rope, and had started to tie the man's legs together. His plan was to lift Borg up by his feet with the aid of a hook secured to the aircraft roof. There were several such hooks fixed to the ceiling of the cargo area, and fortunately, one was directly above the open hatch.

Once the feet had been tied together, he passed the other end of the rope through the hook, and began to haul the man up. With some assistance from Olga, they eventually had Borg strung upside down immediately above the open hatch.

'So now we just cut him loose,' Olga said with a smile. 'And he disappears down the chute.'

Pablo had produced a short knife. The steel blade was sharp. The rope holding up the unfortunate man was made up of several braids. It had been knitted together from many strands to give it the necessary strength. The rope consisted of twenty four strands in total. After examining it for a while though, Pablo suddenly looked up at Olga with an enthusiastic expression.

'How about we play a little game? We can even have a small wager on it.'

'What have you got in mind?' Olga looked a little bemused.

Pablo took hold of the rope, and pushed the blade of the knife in behind one of the strands of rope. Then, with a flick of his wrist, he cut through it. The rope still held, as there were twenty three other individual strands to it. It had only lost a small part of its overall strength.

He looked towards the woman. Even after many hours of being aboard the flight to Jordan, she still looked good. 'So, this is how it works. We each cut a strand of rope in turn. Whoever makes the last cut, before this guy drops down the chute, is the winner.'

Olga laughed. 'And what is the winner's prize?'

'Well, if you win, you get my share of the bonus from this trip.'

The woman nodded her consent. That was a big wager. On her last trip to this part of the world, the figure had been almost two thousand dollars.

'And if you win?'

Pablo grinned. His tongue involuntarily ran along his upper lip. 'I get to fuck you.'

Olga laughed again. 'Are you sure you still have what it takes?'

'Don't worry about me. Is it a bet?'

She nodded, as she took the knife from his hand. 'It's a bet.' Then she leaned forward and cut another strand of the rope. The weight of the man still held.

Borg had been listening to their discussion. He was now in a state of pure panic. Hanging upside down had caused a lot of his blood to run to his head, and he was feeling very unwell. His arms hung lifelessly down below him, and his hands were well inside the chute. He felt sure he could start to feel some movement returning to parts of his body. He could swivel and focus his eyes, which was a marked improvement.

Looking down beneath his head, he could see the long chute and the cover at the other end. The air outside the aircraft was whistling past, and in the enclosed two metre tunnel, the noise was very loud. He had heard the bet being made, and he could feel the strands of rope being cut one by one. The laughter of the man and woman coming from above was driving him mad. Surely they weren't going to let him drop out of the plane. He was a government official, an important man. He would be missed, questions would be asked. Surely they realised this.

Another of the braids had just been cut. He felt the movement, and heard more laughter. That made ten cuts in total now. The rope would be losing a significant part of its strength.

Borg tried once more to move his arms, and to his utter disappointment, they still didn't respond. However, he felt his fingers tingle. Rolling his eyes towards his outstretched arms, he could see some of his fingers bending slowly. At last, he thought hopefully.

He tried to focus all his attention on his hands. Then suddenly, one of them moved and touched the side of the chute. It felt cold and metallic. The other hand was now also moving. All of the fingers on the second hand were now functioning.

There was more of the laughter and he counted another four cuts being made to the rope. Then, the rope seemed to stretch, and his body dropped. It was only half an inch or so, but it was a definite movement. He realised that his time was running out.

Pablo and Olga had seen the sudden drop, as the body of the man pulled against what was left of the rope.

Pablo handed the knife over to the woman. 'Wait a minute. I think it's going to go.' He was watching the rope intently.

'It's holding. And now it's my turn again.'

She pushed the knife in amongst the last few remaining braids, and jerked her wrist. The blade sliced through the section of rope. But it held firm. The body was still being supported. Then, just as she was passing the knife back to Pablo, there was a loud crack and the rope gave way. Borg's body was there in front of them one second, and the next it was gone. The Maltese man went straight down the chute and disappeared from sight.

Borg was just beginning to regain some hope, when he heard the rope snap. His hands were now almost fully functioning as the effect of the chemical in his body was wearing off. As he dropped down the chute, he managed to grab hold of a metal handle protruding from the end of the tube. He gripped it with all his might, but such was the weight of his body falling, that all he managed to do was to completely sever three of his own fingers.

That was the last sensation he remembered before his body shot out of the end of the chute, and into the cold air beyond.

'I win. I win.' Olga jumped with delight. 'This is going to be a very profitable trip for me.'

Pablo stared blankly down the chute. He was feeling acutely disappointed. Not that he cared about his bonus. He was already a relatively wealthy man. Neither was he particularly bothered about the customs official from Malta. The man was an idiot. No, what he was annoyed about was that he had really wanted to make love to the woman. He had been so close to achieving that. It would have been a dream come true.

'When do I get my money?' Olga was still giggling.

'You'll have it just as soon as we get back to Havana. Don't worry, I will pay up. After all, a bet is a bet.'

'Oh dear, it looks like you are a sore loser. You're not going to cry are you?'

Pablo smiled back at her. 'No, I'll get over it.'

'Good,' she said. Then she took his hand and pulled him towards her.

'Because I don't want you looking all sad while you're fucking me.'

Chapter Twenty Four

Cole was sat at a window seat of the Imperial Hotel in Havana. It was just after midday. He looked at the large clock on the wall in front of him, and cursed Hedge for being late.

Cole was ex-army, and he had spent several years with British Special Forces. He didn't like full time work. He enjoyed being a free agent. Occasionally, he was asked to do undercover jobs for the various agencies of the government. He had been carrying out a job for the then British Prime Minister when he had first met his friend Hedge.

That had been a few years ago. Hedge had accidentally been caught up in Cole's investigation into a group known as the Palindrome Cult. He'd had several unpleasant experiences as a result of that. Cole chuckled to himself as he remembered the adventure. His new friend had done well considering he had been totally out of his depth.

Cole checked the clock once more, and then he looked round towards the entrance of the hotel. Just as he did so, a tall, pale-faced man walked into the lobby. The guy had dark brown hair, and looked somewhat nervous. Even though they hadn't met for almost two years, Cole recognised him immediately. He jumped up from his seat and strolled over towards him.

'You must be the only person I know who could spend two weeks in the Caribbean and still look as white as a ghost.'

Hedge scrutinised his old friend. 'And I bet you're the only person in this hotel who's carrying a handgun.'

Cole laughed. 'It's good to see you have remembered some of the things I taught you.'

Then they were both laughing. Some of the anxiety had disappeared from Hedge's expression. They sat down and ordered some drinks. For a while they chatted about old times. The last time they had met was when they were on a road trip across the United States. It was supposed to be a vacation but had ended up as a terrifying experience, particularly for Hedge.

'And how's your sister Maddie?' Cole suddenly changed the subject.

'She's good. We had a great time cruising around the Caribbean.'

'I hear you went swimming out in the middle of the sea.' Cole chuckled when he saw the expression on his friend's face.

'So you heard about that?'

'Always the hero, aren't you?' This comment was followed by more laughter from Cole. 'Didn't Maddie want to come here with you?'

'No. She's already seen Havana. And anyway, I wanted to keep her as far away from you as possible.'

'Why do you say that? I think that's rather unfair.'

Hedge frowned. 'Cole, whenever I meet up with you people seem to get hurt, and even killed.'

Cole shrugged his shoulders. 'Again, that's very unfair.'

Hedge shook his head. 'Anyway, my sister has a job interview back in Houston. She's decided to stay in Texas with her aunt and uncle for a while.'

Hedge went silent for a moment. He took a long gulp from the cold beer in front of him as his mind drifted.

It was an unusual situation, but Hedge hadn't known his younger sister for very long. Maddie had been staying with him in London for a couple of years. She'd enjoyed her time there, and had made many friends. She was very likeable, lively and fun. Her good looks and the easy going American accent gave her a constant stream of admirers.

He thought back to the first time he'd met his sister. It had been in a cemetery on a grey day in Houston, a few years back now. Hedge had just arrived in Texas, accompanied by Cole. The two of them were on a personal assignment for the British Prime Minister.

Even after all this time, Hedge still couldn't believe that he had become caught up in such a dangerous mission. He had diverted to Houston in order to try and find the place where his parents had been buried after the tragedy of their deaths.

He found the graves. He also found Maddie, who he never knew even existed until that day. She was visiting the same cemetery, on that same day. But then, she did visit her parents' graves most days, so it wasn't that much of a coincidence that they had met there.

A few days later in New York, they'd exchanged their life stories over a coffee. It turned out that Hedge's mother had been pregnant with Maddie at the time of the car crash. His mother had died, but Maddie had been born. She had been adopted by an uncle who lived near Houston, in the United States. Maddie told him about her life in Houston. The family she had grown up with were great, even if they were very private people. She had done well in school, and enjoyed playing sports, but her real passion was horses. She had learned to ride from an early age, and spent most of her free time out with her horse. It was strange, she said, not knowing her mum and dad, and that saddened her.

She was a bit confused initially about finding out that she had a big brother, but had now got used to the idea. She wanted to spend a bit more time with her new brother, so had come over to London to stay with him for a while.

Hedge came back to the present with a jolt. Cole was talking.

'So, do you want to know what we've been asked to do, and why we need to start in Havana?'

'Not really.' Hedge genuinely didn't. 'Actually, I'd just like to return to England and get on with my life.'

'Good luck with that.' Cole looked serious for a moment. 'Don't be surprised though, when you arrive back at Heathrow airport, to be dragged off and interrogated by some big, ugly MI5 agent.'

'And they'll do what exactly?' Hedge looked unimpressed. 'I'm a British citizen with certain rights. Even they can't just go around doing what they want to.'

'Unfortunately they can.' Cole was nodding his head. 'I should imagine that within ten minutes of the plane touching down, you will be undergoing a thorough examination of your bags. They will almost certainly find some illegal substances. Then, once a rather unpleasant full body search has been completed, you'll be carted off to spend some quality time as a guest at one of Her Majesty's finest prisons.'

'They can't do that.'

Cole blinked rapidly. 'Are you serious? You don't fuck with these people. I knew a guy who recently decided he didn't want to follow the instructions he was given by these gooks.'

Hedge looked unimpressed. 'And what happened to him?'

'What happened was exactly like I just said. Unlucky for him was that he was put in the same cell as a psychotic sex offender. Even after they heard the guy's continual screams, they still refused to move him to another cell, although they did offer him a large tub of lubricating cream. Don't make the mistake of thinking you have any rights where these people are concerned.'

Hedge winced. The nervous, worried look had reappeared on his face.

'So what exactly have we been asked to do?'

Chapter Twenty Five

Hedge didn't sleep well that night. It was hot in Havana, and humid. He kept the window open all through the hours of darkness so that some of the cool breeze blew in. The trouble was it also allowed in the sounds and smells of the old town. Both were very noticeable and not helpful when he was trying to doze off.

He couldn't stop thinking about the conversation he'd just had with Cole. Despite what had happened on the ship, Hedge wasn't a hero, far from it. He was an anxious person. Was it in his makeup, or had he developed it over time? He wasn't sure. What his old friend had just outlined though made him feel sick to the core. He was trapped, as he had been before. Cole enjoyed these little adventures. Hedge didn't.

There was a small, digital clock on the bedside cabinet next to him. The display told him that it was quarter past three in the morning. The numbers blazed out brightly, so he leaned his hand out and adjusted the brightness control on the side. That was better. The display was now only just visible. There was less light being given off. Hopefully he would now be able to sleep. But was it now too dull? He adjusted the control again, turning up the illumination. No, too bright again. After several more attempts to get the perfect light level, he started to feel stressed, and so he gave up.

He often had these little battles with insignificant things. It was an anxiety issue. He envied other people being able to relax so easily. He sometimes felt that he was in a constant struggle with his emotions. It was difficult to explain, just a feeling that something wasn't quite right. Why did he sometimes feel so uncomfortable?

Where did that come from? He often blamed his school days for these feelings.

Anxiety was a common ailment in society, he knew that. After reading several books on the subject, he was something of a minor expert on it. In the past, he'd seen various therapists, and tried a few techniques to help him manage the problem, but still he resented the unwanted emotions.

Could it really have developed from his time at boarding school? It had all seemed such good fun back then. He had made many friends, and been involved with various sports.

But then, what about all the bullying? Yes, it had been quite bad. In fact, it seemed quite horrific by today's standards. But could that really have been responsible for some of his nervous mannerisms when it was such a long time ago?

As he lay in bed, looking at the curtains blowing gently, his mind started to drift back in time. Back to when he was a young boy at boarding school.

Hedge had been at Upperdale College for about two years, so he must have been around thirteen years old. One evening, just after dinner, a senior boy called Jeremy Potts had given Hedge a large pile of clothes to be washed. This was common practice at the college, and there were many tasks that junior boys carried out for the seniors. It was a form of slavery if you like, but the school masters tended to turn a blind eye to it.

'Make sure you clean them properly, you little shit. Use plenty of soap powder, and don't damage anything. If you do, I'll be charging you for it.'

It was nearly two hours later when Hedge walked up to the second floor of the boarding house and stood outside Potts's room. He knocked on the door gently.

'Piss off, I'm busy,' came the immediate response.

Hedge was unsure what to do. He needed to tell Potts that he had finished the washing, but he didn't want to annoy him. The senior boy had a reputation for being quite violent when he was upset. He knocked again, and spoke through the door.

'I've done your washing. It's hanging up to dry in the laundry room downstairs.'

He waited patiently for what seemed like a long time. There were voices coming from inside the room, but still the door hadn't been opened. Then, suddenly, the door flew open, and Potts stood in the doorway.

'Didn't I tell you to go away?'

Hedge was scared, as the senior boy had a hard, scowling expression on his face. But he managed to blurt out his words.

'I've done your washing.'

'Good. I hope you got those dirty stains out of my underwear. If not, then you can do it all again.'

Hedge nodded. 'Yes, all clean.'

'Okay. Now fuck off and stop annoying me.' Potts was about to close the door to his room, but then appeared to have second thoughts.

'Actually, before you go, we could use someone like you to settle an argument we're having. Come inside for a moment.' Potts laughed, and pulled the junior boy into his room.

As he was being dragged inside, Hedge noticed that there was another senior boy present. Potts said that his friend's name was Bart. He started to explain that the two of them had been having an argument, or rather, a friendly debate about a certain topic. It related to something that Bart thought couldn't be done, but Potts disagreed. They had each bet twenty pounds in hard cash on the eventual outcome.

Hedge listened intently. He had no idea what they were talking about. The two seniors had started arguing amongst themselves, but the junior boy was no longer paying attention. He had caught sight of a tall glass full of liquid. It was sitting on top of a desk in the corner of the room. He couldn't make out what the liquid was in the glass. Bart was pointing towards it as he spoke.

'I still say you couldn't do it without vomiting. I'm happy to raise the bet to fifty pounds if you like.'

Potts was nodding his head. 'Fifty pounds it is then.'

Suddenly the two seniors had stopped their bickering. They were both staring directly at Hedge. He started to feel very nervous.

89

Not just because of the attention of the older lads, he was also still trying to fathom out what the liquid was in the glass.

It was a dark yellow colour, and he thought he recognised that pungent smell.'

Chapter Twenty Six

Potts had picked up the glass and was walking towards Hedge.

'It appears you have saved me from personally proving Bart here completely wrong. You see, one of us is going to have to drink this glass full of piss without throwing up. That way I will win fifty pounds. And guess what, it's not going to be me. I hope you're thirsty young man, as this is all for you.'

Hedge tried to back away from the unpleasant drink he was being offered, but Potts grabbed him by the neck and pulled him closer. The senior boy moved his face so that their noses were almost touching. Hedge could smell the disgusting aroma coming from the liquid, as well as Potts's awful bad breath.

'If you spill any of this then the bet is void, and I lose my money. If you don't drink it all, then I will lose my money. If you throw up after drinking it, then I lose the bet. If any of those events occur, then not only will you owe me fifty pounds, but I will make your life at this school absolute hell for the next year. Do you understand me?'

Potts tightened his grip as he spat out his words. Hedge had now become very concerned. He had no idea how he would be able to find fifty pounds even if he suddenly had to. But what he was really worried about was how he was going to drink what looked like around half a pint of pure piss. And whose urine was it anyway? Where had it come from?

Potts had now pushed the glass firmly into Hedge's right hand, and told him to get on with it.

'I need to go now,' Hedge blurted out. He didn't know what else to say. His voice came out as barely a whisper. 'Please let me leave.' He tried to hand the glass back to the senior boy.

'What the fuck are you talking about? You're not going anywhere yet. First of all you need to have a long drink.' replied Potts.

Bart was laughing now. 'Someone has to drink it or I win the bet. I don't mind who it is. One of you has to disprove my point.'

Potts turned and scowled at Bart. 'This little shit is going to prove that I'm right. There is no way that I'm drinking your urine. But I am going to win that cash.'

Hedge now had the answer to one of his questions. But knowing who had supplied the urine was of no help. Like Potts, he didn't particularly want to drink a glass of piss. It could lead to him getting some kind of illness. He had read somewhere that even though people have survived in the wild by drinking their own urine, it was quite dangerous to do so.

Potts was now getting angry. He turned back to Hedge and shouted at him.

'Get on with it. I need to see you down this. All of it.' He pushed the hand holding the urine back towards Hedge.

The younger lad reluctantly bought the glass up closer to his face. Seemingly he had no choice. As it was just a couple of inches from his mouth he paused. The stench from the vile liquid was horrendous. He could already feel himself starting to gag.

The senior boy looked on. He was leaning close to Hedge and he seemed tense. Clearly he didn't want to lose the bet. There was a lot at stake. Not just money, but it had also become a matter of pride between the two seniors. Potts had his fists bunched. He looked very intimidating.

Hedge moved the glass in closer to his mouth. It was now touching his lips. Tipping the glass over a little more, he suddenly felt the liquid in his mouth. It tasted horrendous. There was a strong salt presence, along with a bitter, almost acidic taste. He swallowed a small amount of the liquid, but then stopped himself pouring any more into his mouth as he felt like he was about to be sick.

'Keep going,' screamed Potts. 'That's only one mouthful. There is still a long way to go.'

Hedge moved the glass back to his lips once more, and trying a new strategy, he quickly drunk down several large gulps. Instantly he regretted doing this as it felt like his throat was on fire, and the urge to be sick was even greater than before. He set the glass down quickly and doubled up, coughing violently as he did so.

Potts immediately picked it up, and pulling him up straight by his hair, he handed the drink back to him.

'That's half of it gone, a few more gulps and you're done. You could yet save yourself a serious beating young Hedge.' There was almost admiration in Potts's voice, but still a hint of menace.

Hedge just wanted to get the ordeal over with now, so he grabbed the glass and drank down the remaining urine in a few quick mouthfuls. It tasted disgusting, but he realised he had to finish this as quickly as possible. Again he bent forward, coughing and retching, but the task was finished, the glass was empty. He tried desperately not to vomit. He straightened up, still coughing, but hopeful that the liquid would stay down. There were a few tears stinging his eyes as he looked towards the senior boys.

Both Potts and Bart were laughing hysterically. They were no longer concerned about the outcome of the bet, but rather it was just hilarious seeing the junior boy's discomfort. They had literally collapsed in a heap on the floor, and were beside themselves with mirth.

Hedge seized the opportunity. While the two older boys were lying on the carpet and slapping each other on the back, he opened the door to the room and bolted out. The nearest wash room was at the end of the corridor, and he ran into it, locked himself in a cubicle, and immediately started vomiting in to the toilet.

It was almost an hour later that he felt it was safe to come out of the cubicle. He walked back to his own dormitory and tried to drown out the lingering taste in his throat with a bottle of strong ginger beer.

Chapter Twenty Seven

The city of Havana is on the Northern side of the island of Cuba. Just over two million people live there, and surprisingly, it is only around one hundred and five miles south of Key West in the state of Florida.

'It's too big a task. We don't even know what we're looking for.' Hedge was sweating slightly. He was also feeling tired and irritable due to the broken, fitful sleep that he had experienced the night before. It was late morning, and the temperature was rising fast. Although not officially hurricane season, there had been a storm pass by the island recently, and the wind was still strong. It helped to keep the heat down, but only a little.

'You could be right about that.' Cole scanned his eyes left and right. The port of Havana covered a big area. There were boats of all sizes constantly moving up and down the channel. Cargo ships, tankers, even cruise ships. All types of vessel were well represented.

Cole turned away from the water and looked back towards the town. 'I need a drink. Let's get out of this sun for a while. We need to think about our next move.'

They walked down a wide road called Avenida de Belgica for about half a mile, then turned off into a smaller side street. The imposing, white building known as El Capitolio was looming up in front of them, when they spotted a small, secluded cafe bar with outside seating and a large awning overhead. They sat in the welcome shade and ordered some cold drinks.

'What sort of boat did he tell you to look out for?' Hedge had been unimpressed with the lack of detail provided to his partner by the FBI contact.

'He didn't really know. It could be anything.'

'Well that's narrowed it down a bit. Let's go back to the port and ask if anyone's seen a floating object arrive there in the last few weeks.'

Cole ignored the sarcasm.

'But surely,' Hedge continued, 'if this gang are trafficking children on a large scale, then they are going to be using some kind of passenger vessel, obviously, not a large one, but maybe something small and inconspicuous'

'Not necessarily. You're assuming they are transporting the kids in some degree of comfort. That's a pretty big assumption.'

Hedge swallowed hard, but said nothing. The thought of young children being taken from their parents and shipped abroad was harrowing. He recalled what he had felt when he had first found out that his parents were both dead. It was a numb, bleak feeling, like your whole life has just crumbled away before you. These youngsters would be feeling totally lost and helpless. They would be frightened and totally vulnerable. He tried to push the sickening thought from his mind.

Cole changed the subject slightly. 'As I told you earlier, I met Laura's mother a few days ago in Gainesville. The poor woman looked like she had been to hell and back. She's an absolute wreck, physically and mentally.'

'Does she have other children?'

'No, she has just the one daughter, or had should I say.'

Hedge winced at that. 'Did she mention the father, back in London, the Education ministry guy?'

'She wanted to know what he was doing to help find her daughter. I explained that I had been sent to help the FBI. That didn't go down well. I think she was hoping for a whole lot more than just one man.'

'You mean two men.'

Cole frowned. 'That sounds a lot better. I'll go back and tell her shall I?'

Hedge ignored Cole's attempt at humour. 'What is the FBI doing about the problem? If it's as big as you say then surely they have a lot of resources assigned to it.'

'They have some resources, yes. But they also have to cover terrorism, gun crime, drugs cartels, and a multitude of other things. Apparently, they are doing their best.'

'So they're doing fuck all about it then.'

Cole shrugged. 'To be honest, I got the definite impression that they see the whole thing as quite a low priority.'

'Are you serious?' Hedge looked shocked. 'So someone is stealing American kids, shipping them abroad, and the Feds aren't especially interested.'

'You have to understand that most of the children involved are from poor, underprivileged and immigrant backgrounds. Either the parents aren't educated enough to know how to get the help they need, or they're too drunk or high to do so. It seems the gang are mainly focusing on those types of people for their supply. I think they realise that no one will make too much of a fuss about them.'

'What about our girl, Laura, she doesn't fit that profile.'

'No she doesn't.' Cole looked thoughtful. 'I have a theory that she was stolen to order. A certain type of girl where age, colour, background all had to be matched.'

'So as regards her, is the FBI interested?'

'They see this one as a British problem. The mother is from England, and the father is a government minister.'

Hedge was quiet for a moment. His brain was ticking. Cole sat silently for a while, sipping his beer.

'So what else did you follow up on in Gainesville? I assume you did all the background checks while you were there, like school, friends, favourite places, medical history, dental records, clubs, hobbies. Did you come up with anything of interest?'

'Very good,' Cole's tone was mocking. 'You're not related to Sherlock Holmes by any chance are you?'

Hedge just stared back at him, but didn't respond.

'Yes, I did all of the above. There was nothing of any consequence. She enjoyed school, had lots of friends, hated playing sports, and was very kind and polite.'

'So pretty normal then. Did you come across anything or anyone unusual?'

Cole thought for a moment. 'Her school headmaster was a rather angry man with awfully bad-smelling breath, the lady at the medical records office was uncooperative and seemed incredibly nervous, and Laura's dance instructor was a gorgeous woman with very large breasts. She invited me back to her apartment later that same day for dinner.'

'So you didn't get very far then?'

'We went all the way actually, although we never got to the dinner.'

Hedge shook his head. 'I meant that you didn't get very much useful information from anyone.'

'No, not really, although after a long discussion with each of the people I met, I did leave them a note of my name and number.'

Chapter Twenty Eight

Ruby Anderson arrived back at her Gainesville apartment just after six o'clock in the evening. It had been a tiring day, and a long one. During the morning a major computer glitch had occurred at the Medical Center, and so accessing patient records had been all but impossible. The nursing staff had given her a hard time, even after she had explained that there was nothing she could do about it.

She opened her front door and stepped inside. Just as she was closing the door behind her, there was a crash against it from the other side, and she felt herself being flung backwards. She landed awkwardly on the floor of her hallway, and the contents of her shopping bag were dispersed across the carpet. A jar of spaghetti sauce smashed as it landed, and a bright red liquid was splattered everywhere. For a moment she thought it was her own blood.

'What the hell,' she screamed, as she tried desperately to force the door shut with her feet.

But it wouldn't close. There was a man standing between the door and its frame. He was of medium height, with ordinary looking, dark brown hair. The guy had unusually deep-set eyes, something Ruby hadn't noticed the last time they'd met. What she did recognise straight away though was the long raincoat.

'You could use the fucking doorbell like everyone else does.' Ruby was now angry as well as tired. 'And I thought we weren't ever going to meet again. Wasn't that one of your rules?'

'But there was another rule as well, don't you remember?' The man looked quite menacing. There were dark shadows around his eyes, which gave him the appearance of someone who might have just risen from a grave.'

'I don't give a shit about your rules, just leave me in peace. I've kept my part of the bargain. And take that bloody coat off. It's hot as hell out there.'

Ruby was on her knees by now, trying to gather up her groceries and put them all back in to the brown paper bag. She was just reaching for a can of baked beans when he stepped forward, and with a sudden, violent movement, he swung his right foot up into her stomach. The pain was intense, and she screamed at the top of her voice. It felt like something had ripped deep inside her, and instinctively she curled up into a ball, struggling for breath.

As she rolled onto her side, the man in the coat lashed out again with his leg. This time there was a soft crunching sound, and a small pool of blood started to form near her face. Ruby's nose had disintegrated under the impact of the man's metal reinforced shoe, and she could feel several of her teeth had become dislodged. Then everything went black and she passed out.

When her consciousness returned, it felt like every nerve in her body was on fire. Her mouth and nose hurt like hell, and her stomach ached badly. But she couldn't even begin to focus on those areas, because what was taking up all her attention was the acute agony coming from both of her shoulders. It felt like her arms were literally being ripped from their sockets. Desperately, she tried to take in her situation. Moving her head slowly from side to side, she realised that somehow she was hanging in mid-air. The rope holding her was tied tightly around both her hands, and the other end had been fixed to the light fitment on the ceiling of her kitchen.

The real problem was that although her body was facing forward, her hands and the rope holding her up were behind her. So her arms were being forced upwards by her body weight, twisting her shoulder joints at an impossible angle.

She screamed in agony, a long, groaning sound. Her moaning was incoherent, as she was struggling to form any words.

There he was again, the man in the raincoat, standing directly in front of her. He lifted his arm and placed it around the back of her neck. In any other situation it would have looked like a friendly gesture. Possibly even someone comforting a troubled friend. But then he started to put downward pressure on his arm. This effectively increased the weight pulling on her arms tied behind her, forcing the shoulder joints into an even more impossible position.

She shrieked loudly. Foamy saliva started to form around her mouth and run down her chin. Her legs were kicking wildly behind her, but this movement just had the effect of putting more pressure on her tortured shoulder muscles.

The man laughed softly. 'Shall we try again with remembering the rules? Now what was it that you weren't going to do?'

Ruby was panting hard, struggling for breath. Her eyes were rolling wildly. The pain coming from the top of her arms was excruciating. The man was talking, but she was struggling to make out what he was saying.

'Help me, the pain. Help,' she spluttered.

The pressure on her neck increased slightly, sending another agonising shockwave across her shoulders.

'Answer my question please. What was the rule?'

'I don't know. Let me down. Please.'

'You weren't supposed to talk about our transaction to anyone. Don't you remember?'

Ruby winced. The pain was becoming unbearable. 'I didn't. I didn't.'

'What about that English man?'

Ruby went silent for a moment. 'Who do you mean?'

The pressure on her neck increased as he pulled his arm down a fraction more.' She wailed in agony again. This time it was a high pitched shriek that seemed to go on forever. At the same time floods of tears were running down her face.

Eventually the wailing turned into a soft moan. The man took the opportunity to ask her again. 'Who was the man from England? What did he want?'

'I don't know. I didn't tell him anything.'

The man with the raincoat shook his head, giving the distinct impression that he was running out of patience. He moved close to her and with his arm still circled around her neck, he lifted his feet up off the ground thereby adding his own body weight to that of hers. This sudden movement increased the pressure on her shoulder joints so much that they were effectively torn apart inside her skin.

The screams from deep within her throat were horrendous. Her body writhed in agony, and her eyeballs looked like they would burst from their sockets. Then, with a sudden, involuntary movement, she threw up. The vile, brown liquid ran down the front of her mouth and stained her shirt. That was the last thing she remembered doing before everything went black once more.

The woman's body was now hanging quite still. With a quick action, the man produced a small, clear plastic bag from his coat pocket, pulled it over her head, and sealed it with a short flexible wire around her neck. He estimated that there would be around three minutes of air available to her.

Moving quickly around her apartment, he pulled open several drawers, and looked in cupboards. From a polished, metal rack next to the television he picked up a large pile of paper and envelopes. He scanned through the various magazines and mail, pausing occasionally to read a certain item in more detail. There were several bills in brown envelopes, and a subscription reminder for Hello magazine. He laughed out loud when he came across some tickets for a luxury holiday in the Bahamas.

'Perhaps you can claim that back on your travel insurance. Hopefully it covers illness, and even death,' he muttered.

Then he hesitated. The next item he had found was a small piece of white card. It was plain on one side, but turning it over, he saw someone had written on it.

'Call me if you can think of anything at all that may be of help. Thanks. Cole.'

Immediately after this was what looked like a telephone number.

From reading the message, he felt confident that the woman had not passed on any information to this man Cole. And she certainly wouldn't be doing so in the future. He put the card in his coat pocket, and threw the remaining wad of paperwork on the floor. Then he walked back into the kitchen and looked at the woman hanging limply. She appeared completely lifeless.

Nodding with satisfaction, he quickly left the apartment, pulling the front door closed behind him.

Chapter Twenty Nine

'We're wasting our time here.'

'I think I have to agree with you.' Cole had lost count of how many hours they had walked around the port area of Havana. They had spoken to several of the cargo handlers working there, but most were reluctant to talk to them. Those who weren't afraid to chat didn't have anything concrete to offer.

'We should head back to Florida. I'm going to meet again with my FBI contact in Miami, and then we can go and talk to the mother once more.'

'Do you think we should be pestering her?'

Cole seemed dejected. 'She's our only link to the girl at the moment.'

They headed back to the hotel and decided to see how soon they could get a direct flight to Miami. Relations between the USA and Cuba had thawed in recent years, and so flying between the two countries was now much easier. And so the following morning they headed for the Jose Marti International airport just outside the capital city, and boarded the short flight to Miami.

The FBI man met them in the arrivals hall.

'Good to see you again Cole.'

'And you. You're looking well. Let me introduce my colleague. Everyone just calls him Hedge.'

The man turned and flashed a generous smile. 'It's nice to meet you Mr Hedge. My name is John Hughes. Please call me John.'

Hedge took his outstretched hand. 'It's my pleasure John, and just Hedge is fine.'

'So are you ex Special Forces also?' The question was genuine from the American.

Cole laughed, and winked an eye at his friend. 'Not exactly, but don't go getting on the wrong side of him. He's a mean bastard when he wants to be.'

Hedge just shrugged but said nothing. If this guy thought he was something special, then that was fine by him.

They headed off in Hughes's black Buick Lacrosse towards the centre of Miami. He left the car in an underground parking lot, and then he guided them across a busy street and into an expensive looking steak restaurant. They sat at the back of the room, away from the crowd. Cole got straight to the point.

'We are going nowhere with this. No one in Havana would speak to us, and I didn't see anything unusual. Are you sure that's the route the traffickers are using?'

'Yes, we're pretty confident of that. We think they are moving them from the port of Miami, but we've searched all over and found nothing conclusive.'

'It's a big port though.'

The FBI man nodded.

Hedge had said very little so far, but he now spoke directly to Hughes. 'Do you have any other leads, anything at all?'

'There are a few things the local police are following up on. One is the blood samples they found at the scene of the girl's abduction. They went over that bus from top to bottom.'

'Surely all the blood was from the mother, when she was attacked with the baseball bat?'

'Well Hedge my friend, ninety nine point three percent of the blood found on that bus did indeed belong to the woman. But, the remaining nought point seven percent did not. That came from someone else.'

'Who is he, or she?' Cole was suddenly interested.

'Who are they?' Hughes replied. 'Across the whole bus, the police identified fourteen separate traces of blood. After all, it is a public vehicle.'

'Not very useful then,' said Hedge.

'On the contrary, we have now eliminated thirteen of those samples as belonging to local people who have used the bus over the last five months. It seems the good folk in Gainesville get injured a lot. We had special permission from the courts to access medical records in order to eliminate potential suspects.' Hughes looked pleased with himself.

Cole swallowed a well chewed mouthful of sirloin steak. 'And the last sample?'

'We think it may belong to the guy with the bat. Apparently several witnesses on the bus said that the young girl was scratching at his face as he tried to grab hold of her. One passenger thought he saw her draw blood. It's now being run through national and international DNA databases. The overseas ones may take some time. But if this guy has a record anywhere, then we will find it, and hopefully him.'

Cole nodded. 'What's the blood group?'

'It's A-positive, quite common unfortunately.'

They finished up their lunch, and promised to keep each other in the loop of any developments. Then Cole and Hedge headed for a vehicle rental office. They planned to drive themselves up to Gainesville.

It was not going to be pleasant meeting the mother again. The last time Cole met her, she was understandably distraught. The idea that her little girl had been kidnapped and shipped overseas had caused her to have a complete emotional breakdown.

Hedge wasn't looking forward to it either.

Chapter Thirty

The woman who opened the door to them looked like a ghost. Hedge and Cole wouldn't have known, but even before her daughter had been taken, she had a very pale complexion. Now she looked white, too white for normal skin. It was probably the prescription drugs, Cole thought to himself. There would be no way for a mother to mentally survive such an ordeal without some kind of strong medication.

She had the top of her left arm in a bandage, and the weight of the arm was supported by a sling which was tied around her neck.

'I hope you were expecting us?' It was all Cole could think of saying. What else could he have opened up with? 'How are you?' would have just sounded ridiculous.

The woman nodded and opened the door wider to let them in. The apartment appeared untidy, with dirty cups and bowls everywhere. The scene in front of them looked like the residence of someone who had lost all hope. Several empty cereal packets had been left casually lying around. A diet of corn flakes and coffee would not be enough to sustain the average person for very long.

Ann McCain was not an average person though. Born in Scotland, and raised in London, she moved to the USA as a one-parent mother shortly after the birth of her daughter. It had taken a lot of courage to start a new life in Gainesville, Florida. She had worked hard at it, and she and her daughter had flourished. Yes, there had been some support from the father. But that was given reluctantly, mainly to avoid a scandal.

But now, her world had been blown apart. 'Child Trafficking' the FBI man had described it to her. 'She's probably

106

been shipped abroad somewhere. That would have happened almost immediately.'

'And that explanation is supposed to help me,' she had screamed at the agent. The man had been completely tactless. Far from helping, it had just served to turn a terrible situation into a fucking nightmare. The thoughts of what might be happening to her six year old daughter left her utterly horrified. Was she being hurt, even tortured? What about sexual abuse? Unthinkable horrors swept across her mind during every waking minute of her day.

Cole had noticed her deterioration even in the few days since he had last met her. Her eyes had completely lost their colour. They were just dark, murky pools. Her hands shook uncontrollably and, when she spoke, she could barely put a sentence together.

'Do you know where ... where she is?' Ann looked towards Cole with a small flicker of hopefulness.

Cole shook his head. Tears immediately started to run down the woman's face.

'But we are not going to stop looking. Me and my friend here will do all we can to find her and bring her back to you.' Cole tried to sound upbeat.

'Promise me you'll bring her back.'

'We will do all we can.' Cole hated to make promises he couldn't keep.

'Promise me.' The woman stared desperately at him. It was a pitiful sight to see.

Hedge sat nervously nearby. He couldn't bring himself to look at the girl's mother. His stomach was churning, and his anxiety levels were at maximum. He pretended to tie his shoelace in an effort to avert the glare of the woman's eyes. After the fourth attempt he gave up. He needed something to concentrate on, but nothing came to mind. So he just stared down at the carpet.

'I will promise you one thing,' Cole said with a hard expression, 'if we find the people who took your daughter, then I will hurt them, badly.'

'Kill them.' Ann McCain stared across at him, but her face showed no emotion. 'Kill them, please.'

Cole nodded. He didn't know what else to do. The hate in the woman's voice had shocked him.

'Say it. Promise me. Find the people who took my little girl, and kill them.' She took hold of Cole's arm as she spat out her words.

Cole looked uncomfortable. He was a hard man, but this woman's soul was screaming out for revenge.

'Say it,' she hissed at him.

'I promise,' he said softly.

They all sat quietly for a short while, lost in their own thoughts. Then Cole turned and faced the woman.

'Ann, can I ask you a question about your daughter?'

Laura's mother stared across at Cole. She looked like she was in a trance. There was no response to his question.

Cole continued anyway. 'Do you know what blood group she is?'

Ann reacted immediately. She jumped up from her chair, shouting hysterically. The previous conversation seemed to have been entirely forgotten. Her short term memory was nonexistent.

'Why are you asking that, is she still alive? Has Laura been injured?' Then she stopped suddenly and slumped back down in the chair.

'Oh my god, have you found a body? Is that why you're asking that?'

'No, we haven't found her yet. We're just trying to gather information about your daughter.'

Ann sat quietly now. Her head was in her hands. She looked completely lost in her own world. Desperation was written all over her face. It seemed to take a massive effort, but she lifted her head up slowly and looked first at Cole and then across to Hedge.

'Please find my little girl. Please. I beg you. Please.'

Hedge nodded back at her. It was all he could manage to do. The woman's plea was harrowing. He felt sick inside.

Cole stood up. 'We'll do everything we possibly can.' He touched the woman lightly on the shoulder, and then they both left the room. All they could hear on the way out was the woman's horrific wailing and her words that echoed around the apartment.

'Laura, where are you, where are you?'

Chapter Thirty One

Laura awoke just as she was being lifted out of the crate.

The man picking her up had a brown face, she noticed. And his breath smelt of fish. She didn't feel very well. Her mouth was dry and she still felt tired, although she must have slept for hours. It seemed ages ago that she had rested her head on the pillow in that strange house. And the top of her arm ached terribly. She looked down at the bandage just underneath her shoulder, and started crying.

Then she remembered her mother, and what had happened to her on the bus. Once again though, as hard as she tried to form the words, nothing came out of her mouth. The man holding her seemed angry. She could understand what he was saying as he was speaking in fluent English, albeit with a strange, foreign-sounding accent.

'The child is filthy. Go and get her cleaned up. And give her some food.'

He passed the girl across to an old woman. She was dressed all in black, and her wrinkled face looked rugged and weather-beaten.

'And see that she is dressed in proper clothes,' the Arab shouted after them.

The old woman told the young girl that her name was Nina. She took Laura to a washroom which was up a short flight of stairs. Once there, she stripped the girl and threw away her old clothes.

For most of the journey Laura had been asleep in the wooden box. She'd woken up a couple of times, mainly when she needed to pee. On both occasions though, as hard as she had tried, she'd been unable to hold it in, and so had urinated through her clothes, and onto the floor of the crate. The dress she was wearing stank badly of stale piss, as did she. She started crying again as she stood naked waiting to be washed.

The old woman slapped her hard on the side of the face. Laura winced at the pain of the smack. Nina spoke very bad English, but Laura could make out roughly what she was saying.

'You not cry. Not cry. This your home now. I your mother now. Your new mother. We look after you. You behave good.'

Laura tried hard to stop crying, but she couldn't. The woman slapped her again. It hurt even more this time.

'Why is this lady so horrible,' she thought to herself. 'What does she mean about being my new mother? I already have a mummy. Where is she?'

Laura turned to face Nina, and tried to ask her to stop hurting her, but the words wouldn't form in her throat. There was something wrong with her voice still, it wasn't working.

The old lady had started to scrub her with an old looking brush. She dipped it into lukewarm water occasionally, then squirted a little green liquid on to the brush, and finally scrubbed Laura all over. When she came to her arms, Nina carefully peeled off the bandage from near her shoulder. It hurt a little as some of the material had stuck to the wound. Laura yelped, and received a slap on her face for it.

The old woman took a soft cloth, wet it, and started to gently rub on the wound at the top of Laura's arm. Eventually it looked clean and tidy. The girl craned her head around to see what was written there. She could see words and numbers, but none of it made any sense to her.

Next, Nina took a short hose and rinsed the girl down with the spray from it. It was cold water and Laura trembled as it splashed against her skin, and ran down on to the floor below. Finally, the woman produced a clean towel and dried Laura with it. Still naked, she then marched her off to a tiny bedroom at the back of the house. It was much smaller than her room at home, and there were no bright pictures on the wall.

'You get dressed,' shouted the woman, as she pointed to a small, black robe lying on the bed.

Laura was acutely aware by now that anything she did to upset this woman resulted in a hard smack on her face. Slowly she walked across to the bed, and pulled the robe over her head. The cloth was hard and itchy, not like her normal clothes.

'You stay here. Wait and pray. Then come down eat. I come get you when ready.' With that said, Nina left the room, slamming the door behind her.

Laura didn't like this place. And she didn't like Nina. She wanted to go home as soon as possible.

She sat on the hard bed and cried. Now that the horrible woman had gone, at least she wouldn't get hit for being tearful.

Chapter Thirty Two

Hedge and Cole left Ann's apartment and walked back to where they'd parked the rental car.

'What next?' Hedge's voice was quiet. He was still suffering from the meeting with Laura's mother.

'We need to call by the Medical Center. I need to ask them something.'

'I thought you'd already been there?'

'Yes, but I want to check on the girl's blood group, if they'll give me that information.'

Hedge looked puzzled. 'Why?'

'Well, my FBI friend seemed to be focused on looking for the man with A-positive blood. But what if it's the girl's blood?'

'Don't you think they'd have thought of that?'

'Maybe they have, or maybe not. It won't hurt to rule it out though.'

They parked up outside the Gainesville Medical Center and headed for the information desk.

'Hello, how can we help you today?' The young lady was polite and smiled pleasantly at them.

'I was here a few days ago, and I spoke to a woman from the records office. I think her name was Ruby. Is she in today? It would be great if I could speak with her again.'

The woman hesitated for a moment. Then she went to say something, but stopped herself. She looked down at the desk in front of her as if she was trying to work out what to do.

'Is there a problem?' Cole sounded a bit too direct. He didn't mean to.

The young lady hesitated a few seconds longer, and then replied slowly. 'I'm afraid that Ruby is no longer with us.'

'Well then can someone else help us please?'

The woman swallowed hard. She seemed to be trying to compose herself. 'What do you need help with? I may be able to be of assistance.'

'I was making enquiries with your friend Ruby about a young girl called Laura McCain. She recently went missing and we are working with the FBI to try and track her down. All we want to know is her blood group. Can you give us that information?'

'I'm not supposed to reveal personal details. I could get myself into serious trouble.'

Cole shrugged.

Hedge stepped up next to him at the counter. 'Could you tell us if her blood group is A-Positive? Surely that's not asking too much is it?'

The girl smiled, and then walked off. She came back a few moments later.

'No, it isn't.'

'Thanks for that.' Hedge smiled back at her and then turned to leave.

The young woman looked at Cole. 'I hope that helps. Is there anything else I can assist you with today?'

'No, you've been great.' Cole turned to go. 'Say hello to Ruby when you see her next, and I hope she is doing well in her new job.'

'Excuse me.' The young woman looked slightly shocked.

'You said she wasn't working here anymore.'

'No, I didn't say that. I said she was no longer with us.'

Cole stopped in his tracks. 'What do you mean?'

'I mean she died'

'I only spoke to her a few days ago. Was she ill?'

'Not that I was aware of.'

Cole frowned. 'Then how did she die?'

The woman took a deep breath before replying.

'Tortured, and then suffocated.'

114

Chapter Thirty Three

'Agent Hughes, are you giving us the run-around here? Did the FBI know that a woman from the medical records office had been killed recently? In fact, very soon after I spoke to her.' Cole was trying not to sound accusing, but he was slightly angry.

'I had come to our attention, yes.'

Hughes had lost some of the friendliness of their former meeting. He didn't like people turning up at his office uninvited.

Cole didn't give a shit that the man was unhappy. 'Did you think that was unusual, or possibly too much of a coincidence?'

'We have people looking into it.'

'And when were you going to tell us about that?'

'We would have passed on the information if, and when, our investigation proved that there was a link to the girl's abduction.'

Cole stayed silent for a while, trying to control his anger. Hughes was hiding something. That was for sure. Maybe he knew more than he was letting on and wanted to take the credit for cracking a major human trafficking ring.

'Do we know anything about the murdered woman, or the person who may have killed her?'

Hughes was abrupt. 'Not at this stage. Her name was Ruby Anderson. I will let you know when we have more to tell. Maybe you should focus on finding the girl. That's what your government wants you to do.'

Cole was seething, but he tried not to show it. 'And you can be sure I'll tell my Prime Minister exactly how helpful you people have been.' He turned to Hedge, who had been sitting quietly next to him. 'Let's go. I think we're done here.'

Once outside the Miami FBI building, Hedge turned to his friend. 'He's trying to sideline us.'

'He's a fucking dickhead.' Cole was still annoyed with the man.

They headed for a nearby Starbucks cafe, found some comfortable seats, and sat down with hot drinks and two chicken wraps. Cole was checking messages on his cell phone, while Hedge ate his food, and stared aimlessly out of the window. The traffic in this part of Miami was heavy as workers were starting to head home after their busy day in the office.

Hedge had started to mumble to himself. Cole was trying to concentrate. 'What are you muttering about?'

'Wait a minute.' Hedge held up a flat hand to him, and carried on talking quietly to himself.

Cole ignored him.

Hedge had closed his eyes by now, and was moving his head slowly from side to side. He looked like he was calculating something. Cole had seen his friend like this before. It appeared to anyone watching closely that he was running scenarios or outcomes through his head. Like a computer might do. Eventually he stopped mumbling, opened his eyes, and looked up.

'That's it, quite obvious really.' He sat back in his seat and took a long slurp of coffee.

'So, go on then Einstein. What exactly is obvious?'

'If you wanted to sell children, what sort would you go for?'

Cole looked confused. He shook his head. 'I've never thought about it.'

'What would you want?'

'A quiet, well behaved one?' Cole said it as a question.

'Good luck with that,' replied Hedge. 'Maybe, but more importantly, you would want a healthy one.'

Cole nodded his agreement.

Hedge continued. 'So you would need to look through medical records, or get someone to do it for you. But they'd want something in return.'

'Some form of payment. But why then kill that person?'

'Because they were seen talking to someone they shouldn't have been talking to.'

Cole nodded again. Now he felt somehow part guilty for Ruby Anderson's death. 'So we need to find who killed her. Difficult if we're not getting any help from our FBI friends.'

It was Hedge's turn to nod his head. 'Yes, we could try and find who the killer is. Or, we could just find who made the payment. That sounds much simpler.'

'You think so?'

Hedge smiled. 'I'll bet money that the payment to her was an international bank transfer. Where's the global banking centre for much of the world? London. And I know someone not sitting very far away who has friends in high places in that particular city. You need to make some calls. You're asking for details of an international payment made to a Mrs Anderson of Gainesville, Florida, in the last few weeks.'

Hedge had a smug expression on his face. He couldn't help it.

Cole noticed. 'You think you're fucking clever don't you?'

Hedge didn't reply.

Cole got up from his seat and went outside to make some calls.

About fifteen minutes later he came back inside the cafe and sat down. His coffee had gone cold, so he ordered another.

'I should get some information within an hour.'

'You have friends in high places indeed.' Hedge was impressed.

Forty two minutes later Cole's cell phone buzzed briefly. He looked down at the incoming message. Then he glanced across at Hedge, and a smile spread across his face.

'Even better than I'd hoped for. A small payment was made to a Mrs. Ruby Anderson just a few days ago. Guess where the originating bank is based?'

'Cuba.'

'Smart arse,' Cole looked disappointed. He was hoping the answer would be a surprise. 'There's more though. The same bank is making lots of miscellaneous, large payments to other US based accounts. This is obviously a big operation. It wasn't easy to trace, but there are incoming payments to the account in Cuba as well. Many of these exactly match the outgoing transfers.'

'So the Cuba activity is really just a holding account? Where are the incoming payments originating from?'

Cole was still reading the message on his phone. 'All over the place, but there's only one exactly matching amount for the payment made to Ruby Anderson.'

'Where does that originate from?'

Cole looked up from his phone.

'It's from Amman, in Jordan.'

Chapter Thirty Four

Cole made a quick phone call and managed to secure two seats on a flight to Amman the following morning.

'Those goons back in London are paying for this, so I've booked first class. I'd love to be watching their faces when they see that expense line on the monthly statement. They'll probably ask for the credit card back.'

Hedge shrugged his shoulders. 'Well it's a long flight, so we should go in comfort.'

'And we have a short stop in Doha, in Qatar. That will add to the travel time.'

Hedge didn't respond. He was deep in thought. What they had been told about the woman called Ruby had shocked him. 'Tortured and suffocated,' her friend had said. It didn't bear thinking about. And then that latest meeting with agent Hughes. The man had appeared to be quite helpful when they'd first met. But now, he seemed slightly evasive. Maybe he was under pressure from his superiors?

Cole suggested they get an early night, so they headed back to the hotel.

The following morning they checked out and then headed west from downtown Miami towards the International airport. The journey was only a few miles, but the traffic was heavy and so they allowed plenty of time in case of hold ups.

Cole was driving, and he turned off the Dolphin Expressway looking for NW 37th Avenue. The navigation system on the car was telling him that was the quickest way to the car rental office. They would drop off the vehicle there before heading to the airport terminal.

They were now driving north past the Melreese Country Club. It was a warm day, visibility was good, and the views over the golf course were impressive.

Hedge sat in the passenger seat. 'Great scenery, but what is that irritating noise I keep hearing?'

'That will be your brain whirring. You need to chill out a bit more.' Cole turned towards his companion and chuckled.

'Can you seriously not hear that?' Hedge sounded annoyed.

Cole shook his head. 'I can't hear a thing.' Then he lowered the window next to him, and stuck his head out of the car. 'No, still nothing.'

He was about to put the window up, when he stopped himself. 'Wait a minute. Are you referring to that buzzing noise?'

'Yes, and it's getting louder.'

Cole slowed the car, and leaned his neck out of the window a little further. 'You might be right. It feels very close to us.'

Hedge had turned in his seat and was staring intently out of the rear window of the car. He was looking at an object hovering in the air just behind them. 'I can see what it is. It looks like a small aircraft, very small in fact. It seems to be following us.'

Cole had spotted it also. 'It's a drone. Or more like a mini-drone. Someone is trying to keep an eye on us. Let's see if we can lose it.'

With that, Cole pushed his foot down on the accelerator and the car sped up. They could now see the airport on their left, but they carried on driving past it, trying to lose the drone.

'Those things are not supposed to operate near airports. Maybe it will back off soon.'

Cole was concentrating on driving, but he stole a glance in his rear view mirror. The buzzing object was still tracking them. 'That doesn't seem likely to me. The bloody thing is still with us.'

They turned the car off the main highway and made a few quick changes of direction, but still the drone followed. It looked like a radio controlled aircraft of some sort, about a yard long, with two propellers powering it.

Finally Cole gave up trying to lose it, and he pulled the car off the road onto a small driveway that ran down to a disused garage. 'If we can get that garage door opened, we can hide up in there for a while until that thing gives up on us.'

He stopped the car in front of the untidy looking building, and indicated that Hedge should get out and open the large, metal door in front of them. Hedge jumped out and quickly tried to force open the garage door. It was futile though, as the metal had corroded around the edges and become stuck to the door frame.

'I can't move it,' he shouted back to Cole.

'Leave it,' Cole suddenly screamed at him. He was getting out of the car himself, and had a concerned look on his face. The drone was now close to them, and was attempting to land itself next to their vehicle.

'Run. Get out of here.' Cole's voice was full of urgency and panic. 'That thing has got what looks like a bomb strapped underneath it.'

He sprinted towards Hedge, grabbed him by the arm, and pulled him behind the brick building. Within seconds of them both dropping to the ground, there was a loud explosion next to the car. The building protected them from the blast, but when they went back to inspect the damage, their rental vehicle was a burning wreck.

Cole shook his head slowly as he studied the remains of the car. One side of it had been completely destroyed, and thick, black smoke was pouring from it. 'Well, that saves us the job of taking it back to the rental office.' He looked across at his friend. 'Are you okay? That was a bit too close for comfort.'

Hedge just nodded, as he felt unable to speak. His hands were trembling, and he had a look of pure terror on his face.

'You look like you need a drink.' Cole was now smiling. 'Maybe we could get you something a little stronger than tea?'

Hedge didn't respond. He was still staring at the burning vehicle.

'Let's get going,' said Cole. 'We have a flight to catch. Anyway, we need to get away from here, as it appears you have upset someone.' He started to walk off in the direction of the airport.

Hedge turned his eyes away from the wreckage, and followed him a few paces behind. He was shaking his head from side to side. Cole seemed to be finding the whole incident rather amusing, which was annoying Hedge somewhat. If he could have stopped himself from shaking, he would probably have punched Cole in the face.

By the time they'd walked the short distance to the airport terminal, Hedge had managed to shake off some of the shock he was feeling. 'Who do you think was behind that then?'

Cole shook his head. 'I'm not sure, but that's a highly technical piece of kit. And it would need an experienced operative to fly it like that. Someone clearly wants us out of the way.'

'Could it be linked to the death of the Anderson woman?'

Cole nodded. 'Possibly. This trafficking gang must be more sophisticated than I thought. Maybe they think we are on to something. That's a good thing then.'

Hedge was still trembling, and feeling rather unwell. 'Or a bad thing,' he said quietly.

Chapter Thirty Five

The flight to Amman was over twelve hours long, including the stopover. Hedge and Cole had both had a few drinks, again courtesy of the MI5 credit card, and they were hoping to try to blank out the car explosion incident.

Cole had spent most of his time on board trying to chat up the attractive hostess who was looking after them in the first class section of the plane.

'Will you stop pestering her? She's clearly not interested in you.' Hedge had just eaten a very good lunch, and now just wanted to get some sleep.

'Did you know that her name is Amanda?' Cole asked his companion.

'So, who cares?'

'Didn't you once tell me that your first love was a young lady called by that very same name?'

Hedge smiled to himself. It was true, albeit a long time ago now. 'I don't remember that,' he lied.

'Sure you remember it. No one forgets their first time.'

He waved Cole's unwanted attention away, and settled down in his reclined chair for a snooze. As he closed his eyes, he tried not to think about her, but the image of her was suddenly there. Clear and vivid, as if it was only yesterday, the lovely young woman he had met while he was a senior boy at Upperdale college.

Cole was clearly in a childish mood. Leaning over towards his companion, he whispered softly, 'Amanda, Amanda.'

Hedge tried to ignore him, but now Cole was stroking Hedge's arm with his hand. 'I love you Amanda.' Then he burst out laughing.

Hedge flicked open one of his eyes and turned his head towards the irritation. 'Will you kindly fuck off and leave me alone.' He tried to sound serious, but his voice betrayed the fact that he partly enjoyed the humorous distraction. Anything that took his mind off being blown to pieces was useful right now.

Eventually Cole grew bored with his teasing. Hedge turned in the seat, trying to clear his mind. But now he couldn't stop thinking about Amanda. Then, he was back there, all those years ago, back at college as a young man. The thoughts turned into a dream as he slowly drifted off to sleep.

It was a Sunday afternoon and Mr. Simms, a Science teacher at the college, had called Hedge into his office to ask him to run an errand for him. He was to go and find Miss Grey, and give her a letter. Hedge knew who Amanda Grey was. She was a young, incredibly attractive teacher who had recently arrived at the college. She taught English, mainly to the junior boys, and she was Simms's girlfriend.

Hedge took the letter from Simms and headed off in the direction of the staff lodgings. He walked at a brisk pace and arrived at the staff apartments about ten minutes later. Although he knew who Amanda was, he was still quite nervous. She was indeed attractive as Simms had said, and she seemed to be a confident young lady. He guessed she would have been in her mid-twenties, and Simms was probably several years older.

Hedge wasn't used to speaking to female staff members. He was always a little shy in front of women, even more so when they were that much older than he was. For some reason it was worse when they were good looking, but he wasn't quite sure why. As he approached the staff residence, he started to feel anxious.

He pushed open the main door to the block and headed up to the first floor as Simms has directed. Amanda's room was number twenty two and he found it quite easily. He knocked at the door.

He was tense, and kept looking left and right down the corridor to make sure no one saw him. After a few moments the door opened and Amanda stood in front of him.

'So what have we here then? What a handsome young man you are. What's your name?'

Hedge felt embarrassed and his face suddenly turned quite hot.

'Mr. Simms has sent me to find you and give you this letter,' he replied hesitantly.

He held out his hand containing the white envelope. 'He wants me to let him know if there is any reply for him.'

'Well that's nice isn't it, but what does it say in the letter? Did he say?

Hedge shook his head. 'I don't know Miss.

'Come in for a minute, while I read the letter.'

Amanda looked gorgeous as usual, and he noticed that her hair was slightly wet, and that she was wearing her dressing gown. She looked like she had just come out of the shower. She took hold of his arm and pulled him into the room.

'Did I hear that you had a birthday recently, young Hedge?'

He was amazed that she knew that. He stuttered his answer. 'Yes indeed, I was seventeen just a few days ago.'

She turned towards him and smiled, she looked playful and mischievous. As he stared across the room, her face changed to a more serious expression, and her small mouth opened slightly. She looked at him directly and as she did so she untied the cord of her dressing gown. The top opened up and he caught sight of her breasts. Her skin was smooth and white, and the soft, pink nipples stood out from her small mounds.

He couldn't take his eyes off her.

She looked sensational. Amanda moved towards him. 'You can touch them if you like.'

She took hold of his hands and placed them gently on her breasts.

'Squeeze them,' she ordered.

He moved his hands over her soft skin, stopping in the middle of each breast to play with the hard nipple. She had closed her eyes *by now, and was running the tip of her tongue along her mouth. He felt the urge to kiss each of her nipples and so he bent his head down to do so.*

'Well Master Hedge, it seems you have done this before. Keep doing that, it feels lovely.'

He kissed and then sucked each of her nipples a few more times.

She pulled his head away from her chest and kissed him gently on the lips. As she did so, she pushed her tongue deep into his mouth. He responded by caressing her tongue with his own.

She broke her lips away from him, but continued to kiss him around his neck and ears.

As she leaned in close to him, she whispered softly, 'Have you ever made love to a woman?'

He shook his head. He was suddenly very nervous. She seemed so much older and more experienced than him.

She backed away, peeled the dressing gown off and dropped it on the floor. Now she stood in front of him, naked apart from her small, white panties. He stared at her in amazement. She was lovely. Her legs were lean and smooth, and his eyes followed them all the way up to where the soft, white material of her underwear covered her secret parts.

She moved back towards him and slowly started to remove his clothes. His trousers and shirt came off easily. She tried to pull down his underwear, but his erection was making it difficult for her. They came off eventually, and she leaned forward and bit his penis gently.

He was intensely aroused, and was trying hard not to get overexcited. He had heard stories about premature ejaculation, and definitely wanted to avoid anything like that happening to him.

Although only twenty four, Amanda was no beginner when it came to sex. She was wise enough to know that he was dangerously close to climax. It was a great feeling for her to know that she could raise him to such levels of excitement by doing just a few simple things. She wanted to continue to arouse him, but only so far. It was his first time, and she would like him to remember it.

She told him to kneel down in front of her and pull off her panties. He knelt on the floor, and gently started to ease her underwear down. Her skin looked so soft when he was up close. He wanted to touch her, but held back as could feel his arousal rising to an uncontrollable level.

'Do you like it like that? I've shaved it smooth. Run your tongue over my skin and see what it feels like.'

He finished removing her underwear and returned his gaze to the silky skin around the area at the top of her legs. He leaned forward and ran his tongue gently across her.

'It feels lovely,' he said.

She pulled away from him and walked off towards the bed.

'Follow me,' she instructed.

He walked after her. The bedroom was small and sparsely furnished, and had a large double bed close to the window. She was now lying on the bed, and she looked across at him and beckoned him over with the curl of a finger.

He walked over and sat on the edge of the bed. He felt like he could erupt right then and there. She looked so wonderful, so inviting.

'Lay on top of me, gently.'

As he did so, she leaned down and guided him inside her with her hand.

She was very wet, and he slipped into her easily. He pushed himself inside as far as he could. It felt incredible. He looked down and then kissed her gently on the lips. She responded and pushed her tongue into his mouth once more. He started to move his hips up and down. Although this was all new to him, somehow it seemed the natural thing to do. The trouble was that he was so very close to his climax.

'Very slowly,' she said. 'Let me come first. Just very gentle movements, but push hard against me.'

He did what she asked. Making small movements was difficult as he just wanted to thrust hard. He pushed against her and she responded. She was breathing very fast now. They moved slowly for a little while. Slow and gentle at first, but then she was pushing harder against him, while he was concentrating and trying to hold on to his orgasm.

'Don't come yet. I'll tell you when you can,' she whispered.

They continued to move even more slowly. Suddenly she thrust up hard against him and she cried out. 'Oh yes, yes, that's it, yes.'

There was one final, slow push against him, and then she lay still.

She held on to him very tightly, as her breathing started to return to normal.

A few moments later, she took hold of his ear lobe with her teeth and bit gently. 'Now it's your turn, Master Hedge.'

He was aroused to what seemed like an impossible level. He felt sure that he could orgasm without even moving. He pulled out of her slowly and thrust hard down inside her. He started to repeat this a second time, but before he had even started to push back inside her, he was ejaculating.

'Oh my god,' he shouted, as he clenched his eyes shut and held his breath.

He pushed hard into her a few more times before he eventually collapsed on top of her. He could feel his heart beating loudly against her body, and he was breathing heavily.

'Hey, you're squashing me,' she said.

'Sorry, sorry,' he blurted out.

'Well Master Hedge. I do hope you enjoyed that'.

She kissed him tenderly on the cheek, and slipped off the bed.

Hedge got dressed and then paid a quick visit to her bathroom.

When he returned, she took his hand and led him to the front door. 'Try not to get seen by anyone on the way out.'

He smiled at her, and walked off down the hallway. He took just one glance back at the lovely Amanda. She was staring after him, and she waved as he looked back. He knew then that he would remember her forever. His first proper sexual experience, and the first time he had been in love.

Hedge jumped in his seat slightly as he awoke. The overhead announcement was advising passengers that the plane would be landing at Amman in around thirty minutes. Therefore anyone who wanted to use the toilets one final time should do so now.

'Do you mind getting up? I need to go for a pee.' Cole was in the window seat, and Hedge was blocking his access to the aisle.

'I can't get up just at the moment. You'll have to wait.' Hedge turned his face towards Cole, grinning as he did so.

Chapter Thirty Six

Amman was a strange place. It was busy, but not in the way a western city might be. The traffic wasn't so bad, but there were lots of people bustling about. It was modern, with many smart new tower blocks, but also quite bland in other areas. Most of the buildings were several storeys high, and they were an off-white colour that is so common in the Middle-East.

Hedge and Cole took a taxi to the hotel they had booked, checked in, and then immediately headed out into the city. Cole had arranged an appointment at the British embassy, where they were to meet up with a man called Wilkinson. He wasn't sure if he was with the diplomatic staff, or with British intelligence. It wasn't always easy to tell. Lines often became blurred.

The embassy building was in a road simply called Damascus, in the central area of the city. They were shown into a waiting area and offered cold drinks.

'We work on political, aid, commercial, security and economic interests between the UK and Jordan. It doesn't say anything about finding missing children.' Hedge was reading from a glossy pamphlet which he had been given on the way in.

'Not likely to, is it. Importing young girls from the west isn't something you necessarily want to advertise. Anyway, we don't know for sure that she's here. It's just the money that came from Jordan.'

Wilkinson arrived within a few minutes, introduced himself, and then led them into a small meeting room. He was a middle-aged, fit-looking man, with short cropped hair.

'I'm pleased to meet you, and on behalf of her majesty's government I would like to offer our services to you. We will help in any way we can. I am on the embassy staff here, so if you need anything then I will be your contact. I have been briefed on your task. It sounds like a needle in a haystack job to me.'

Cole thanked him, and smiled. He guessed that the man was probably army intelligence, attached to the embassy here. But, what the hell, it didn't really matter who he was.

'Are you aware that we are operating outside of normal channels? I was instructed by a Senior Cabinet Minister, and the Prime Minister is being kept informed.'

Wilkinson nodded. He was well aware. It was a difficult situation for him. Any assistance he provided would be unofficial, but he couldn't hinder the two men's progress in any way. And he definitely wasn't allowed to upset the Jordanians.

Cole continued. 'In that case, we need three things from you. Firstly, a letter of introduction to the manager of the Jordanian National Bank main branch here in Amman.'

Wilkinson nodded again.

'Secondly, I'd like a small bottle of this substance delivered to my hotel room. A few doses should do. I'd go out and get it myself, but I wouldn't know where to begin around here.' Cole handed the man a small slip of paper. There wasn't much written on it apart from a few numbers and letters arranged in a particular format.

Wilkinson, turned the slip up the right way, and smiled briefly. It looked to him like a chemical formula, one that he recognised. 'Can I ask you what this is for?'

'No, you may not.'

'Okay, fair enough. I'll see what I can do.'

'And finally, my colleague and I need some weapons. A couple of handguns will do, something simple, and clean, from a reputable supplier. We may run into some bad people.'

Hedge was about to protest. He hated guns, and Cole knew it. On their first mission together Hedge had shot and killed a young woman. He had to, as Cole was in grave danger at the time. Hedge had probably saved his friend's life. That didn't really help to alleviate the trauma of the event though. He still had terrible nightmares, reliving the moment the woman's chest had exploded in front of him as the bullet had entered her body. He shuddered at the thought.

Hedge returned to the present. Wilkinson was replying. 'I had anticipated you asking that. If you are caught by the local authorities in possession of firearms, I'm afraid that I won't be able to help you. They have some interesting punishments here for things like that. You'd be lucky to get away with having one of your hands cut off.'

Cole laughed. 'As long as we get a choice of which one, I'd prefer to keep my right hand if possible.'

He looked across at his friend. Hedge was trembling slightly, and had turned pale. 'That's not funny Cole.'

Wilkinson passed a business card across the table. 'Go and see this man. He will help you. Take care though. This isn't London or New York. They have different rules here. And take this as well.'

The embassy man held out a small package. Cole opened it quickly to reveal a wad of Jordanian bank notes.

'That should cover all your expenses while you are here.'

Wilkinson wished them well, and then ushered them out of the building.

'Let's go and get some shooters.' Cole laughed out loud, and then slapped his friend on the back.

Hedge was suddenly desperate to go to the toilet.

Chapter Thirty Seven

Laura spent the first three days in her new home doing very little. The only person who spoke to her was Nina, the old woman. Each time they met Nina would remind her 'I your mother now.'

She tried not to cry when anyone else could see her, but when she was alone, especially at night, she cried most of the time. Talking still didn't seem to work for her. Occasionally she had tried to say something to Nina, but no words came out. So she gave up. It didn't matter anyway. She didn't like any of these new people. And she didn't like this new house. And it was far too hot all the time.

They still hadn't given her any proper clothes. All she wore every day was the uncomfortable, long black robe. She thought about trying to run away. But where would she go? Outside the window it looked just like loads of old houses, and lots of dusty ground.

And where was her real mother? She lay on her bed and started to cry again.

There was a gentle tap on her bedroom door. Laura sat up on her bed and wiped her eyes. It mustn't look like she had been weeping. Nina always slapped her hard across the face if she suspected that.

Then there was another tap on the door, this time followed by a quiet voice. It sounded like a young girl. Laura was about to ask who was there but remembered that her voice no longer worked properly. Instead, she walked over to the door and slowly opened it.

'Hello, you must be Laura. My name is Hala. Can I come in?' The small girl spoke perfect English, and in a very polite tone.

Laura nodded, and pulled the door open a little more.

Hala looked left and right down the corridor. There was no one else about, so she entered the room and pulled the door shut behind her.

The small girl sat on the bed and then took a white, cotton cloth out of the pocket in her robe. The material fell open revealing several pink and white coloured chunks. Laura thought they looked like sweets.

'It's called Turkish Delight. Try some.' Hala offered a piece to Laura.

It tasted very sweet, but Laura liked it. While she ate, she studied the small girl carefully. She had a brown face, not as dark as the man she'd met when she first arrived, but similar. The girl wasn't very tall. Her dark hair fell down to the top of her shoulders, and she was dressed all in black. The same type of robe as Laura was now wearing.

Hala looked frail. Maybe she didn't eat enough, Laura thought. Or perhaps she ate too many sweets. Her mother, her real mother that is, was always telling her that eating sugary things was bad for you, and wouldn't help you to grow.

Hala offered her another sweet, but Laura shook her head.

'You don't say much, do you? In fact, you haven't said anything at all since I entered your room. Can you speak?'

Laura shook her head.

'Well I can, so I'll tell you some things about me.'

Hala talked for several minutes, in between finishing off the Turkish Delight. She told Laura that she was eight years old, although most people said she didn't look big enough to be that age. While she didn't actually go to school, there was a really nice lady who visited the house several times a week to give her lessons. Her family had always lived in Jordan, but had only recently moved to be near the capital city. Apparently all the best medical facilities are here in this part of the country.

She explained to Laura that as well as her mother and father, she also had two brothers. They were both older, quite a bit older. One of them actually went to the university in Amman, which was a good achievement. You had to be clever to go there, and you had to have a wealthy family as the fees were high. Luckily, Hala's father was a good businessman, so he was relatively well off.

Laura held up her hand as if to stop Hala from speaking further. She leaned forward and tried to whisper something, but no noise came from her throat. Giving up on that, she simply held up her right hand and pointed to herself. At the same time she shrugged her shoulders.

Hala realised what she was asking. 'You want to know why you are here. Of course you do, that's only natural. Well, when I was very ill recently my father asked me what I wanted more than anything in the world. I told him that I would really like a friend. Someone my own age, and who spoke good English. Someone we could keep forever.'

Laura looked horrified. She was shaking her head.

Hala had jumped up off the bed. She had a big smile and was beaming from ear to ear.

'So you are my new friend. I like you. And I'm going to keep you.'

Laura started crying again.

Chapter Thirty Eight

'This is the place.' Cole was holding a basic map of the city. He looked up at a non-descript and dirty, white building. He took out the card that Wilkinson had given him and checked the address. 'Yes, this is it.'

He walked up a short set of stone stairs, and banged on the heavy, wooden door. The intercom next to him crackled into life.

'How may I help you today?'

'My name is Cole. I have come to buy some goods. I think you may be expecting us.'

There was a short delay, and then the door opened slowly. The inside of the house was clean and tidy. It had been well decorated, and expensive ornaments and trinkets were scattered everywhere. Cole was no expert, but he recognised good quality Chinese vases when he saw them.

The man who answered the door to them was small and thin. He certainly didn't look like your average arms dealer, Cole thought. The man noticed the item that his visitor was staring at.

'It's a turquoise glazed, gourd style, Chinese vase. I believe it's from around the year 1700, give or take a decade. The last time I had it valued it was estimated at ten thousand of your American dollars.'

'Not my American dollars. We're both British. Well, actually, he's American, sort of. But that's another story.' Cole looked across at Hedge, but then turned back to face the Jordanian.

They moved into a larger room and all sat down in comfortable chairs.

Cole came straight to the point. 'We need some weapons, small, but effective. What can you supply us?'

The man sat motionless for a short while. Eventually he got up and left the room. When he came back he was holding a single handgun. Cole recognised it immediately. Weapons training had been his speciality in the army.

'Looks like a Glock G30. I believe the calibre is 0.45, and a standard magazine of ten rounds.'

'That's very good, and almost correct. This is the Gen4 version.'

'May I see it?' Cole held out his hand.

'Do you mind if I see your money first.'

'Sure.' Cole held out a large bundle of Jordanian Dinar notes. 'I think there is around one thousand dollars worth here.'

'I would have preferred actual dollars.' He took the notes anyway.

'For that we want two of these. May I look at it' Cole held his hand out again.

The Jordanian turned suddenly, and walked over to a table. There was a drawer underneath it, which he opened and placed the money inside. After closing the drawer, he spun around. The gun was held in front of him. His eyes looked black and menacing.

'And now you will leave my house, or I will call the authorities.' He waved the gun towards the entrance they came in.

'And our money, we would like to leave with our money.'

The man ignored Cole's demand. He was still pointing the gun at his chest. 'Please leave now.'

Hedge was terrified. He desperately wanted to get out of that place. After taking a few paces backwards, he turned and moved quickly towards the front door. Cole followed. The Glock was still pointing at him. Hedge was just reaching for the door handle, when he heard a thump behind him, followed by a loud crashing noise. He ducked down instinctively, and turned to see what was going on.

The Jordanian man was lying on the ground in his hallway. Blood was seeping from his nose, and littered all around were jagged pieces of broken, turquoise pottery. Cole was holding the pistol. Somehow he'd managed to overpower the man.

'Go and get our money back, while I keep an eye on this idiot.' Cole looked at Hedge for a split second as he spoke. But it was enough. The man on the ground pulled a second Glock G30 from his pocket and was aiming it towards Cole.

'Look out.' Hedge had spotted the movement.

Cole turned and fired instinctively. The bullet tore into the throat of the Jordanian, and exited out of the back of his head. The noise made by the shot in the confined space of the house was horrific. The whole neighbourhood would have heard it.

'Grab the money and let's go.'

Cole picked up the other weapon and stuffed both of them into his trouser pockets.

Hedge quickly retrieved their cash, and then they both left the house. A small crowd of men had gathered on the street outside, wondering where the noise had come from.

Hedge and Cole ignored them, and walked quickly away.

Chapter Thirty Nine

Hedge was feeling agitated. The recent shooting incident had affected him badly. Once they had returned to the hotel, he told Cole that he needed to go and lie down. Cole said that was a good idea, they should keep a low profile for a while anyway.

Hedge felt horribly anxious. Trying to sleep didn't help, it just gave him nightmares. But eventually, he did manage to drift off. He tossed and turned in his bed, and woke up sweating on several occasions. His mind wandered as he slept. He dreamed about being back in London, then about an old girlfriend. Various random images kept flashing across his mind. They were typical of the kind of flashbacks he associated with being anxious. It was a 'chicken and egg' thing. The original incidents had probably kicked off much of his anxieties, but now when he felt worried, the memories would flood back in.

At one point he woke up feeling thirsty. He quickly poured himself a glass of water and went straight back to his bed to lie down. He was still feeling agitated, and his mind was racing. Eventually he drifted off to sleep again. While he dozed, his mind started to relive an old, unpleasant memory all the way back from his school days.

All the students at Upperdale College were getting excited. It was only a few days now until the Christmas holidays. The whole school would shut down for three weeks. Some of Hedges friends were going skiing in Austria and Switzerland He was looking forward to spending some time in London. He enjoyed the buzz and party atmosphere around the capital at this time of the year.

A few of the boys had been playing rugby. One afternoon of each week was set aside for sports training. But now it was almost five o'clock, time to head back to the boarding house and get changed ready for the evening meal.

'I'm going to grab the shower first,' Hedge shouted to his friend as he ran up to the top floor of the building.

'Okay that's fine,' came back the reply. Tim Baker was the same age as Hedge, but quite a bit shorter in height, and not as fit. Although he kept trying for the rugby team, he was never quite up to the required standard.

'You need to bulk yourself up,' the sports coach had advised him.

Hedge reached the top of the stairs well ahead of Baker. The junior boy's room was on the third floor, so there were a lot of steps to climb up.

Just as he was collecting his towel and soap from his bedside locker, Hedge was interrupted by three senior boys. They were in their last year at Upperdale, so they only had a few days left at the school. Their mood seemed very jovial. Hedge thought he smelt a waft of alcohol as they approached him.

'What are you doing back from rugby training so soon?' Andy Adcock was not normally one of the bad seniors, but his tone seemed harsh and angry. Hedge wondered if he might be drunk.

'Training has just finished. I'm going to get myself cleaned up.'

One of Adcock's friends was eyeing up the inside of Hedge's cabinet. 'What's that in there? Are you concealing a bar of chocolate?'

'But we're allowed snacks in the dormitory.' Hedge tried to sound confident.

'Give me the chocolate bar.'

Hedge did as he was told. It certainly wasn't worth arguing over.

Then, without any warning, Adcock bunched his fist and punched Hedge full in the stomach. Hedge doubled up instantly, and started to gasp for breath. The strike had caught him completely by surprise.

140

'Have you got any money?' Adcock's tone was still menacing. Now that he had felt how half a bottle of Vodka made him feel, he wanted to buy some more. Unfortunately, being close to the end of term, he had used up all his cash.

Seeing the junior shaking his head just riled him up even more. Adcock pointed to his two colleagues as he gave out his order.

'Grab hold of this little shit. Follow me.'

The two older lads took hold of Hedge's arms and dragged him back towards the way he had come, in the direction of the top of the stairwell. As they arrived they stumbled across Baker, who had come up the stairs after Hedge and had been spending a couple of minutes getting his breath back. He was still wheezing lightly.

'Hedge, sit down over there.' Adcock pointed to a corner next to the top of the stairs. 'Baker you little squirt, get over here. Do you have any money on you?'

Baker looked terrified. He shook his head slowly.

Adcock nodded towards his two friends. 'Turn him upside down. Let's see what falls out of those bulging pockets of his.'

The other two senior boys hauled the lad up by his feet. They held his legs high in the air. His head was only a few inches away off the hard floor of the landing. As they shook him, he wailed loudly. He didn't like the feeling of the blood rushing to his head, and the older boys grip on his legs was hurting.'

Adcock kicked him hard in the back. 'Shut up. You'll attract attention to us.'

Baker went quiet, all they could now hear was his gentle sobbing.

Adcock started to gather up the few objects that had been ejected from the boy's pockets. There was a half eaten toffee bar, and a used tissue. A small magnifying glass had dropped onto the floor, but now had a crack across its diameter, rendering it all but useless. A few coins rolled around, but in total they didn't even add up to one pound.

'There must be more than this. Hang him over the side, and then give him a shake.'

The two seniors holding the sobbing boy weren't quite sure what Adcock meant. The one nearest to him asked the question. 'What do you mean, over the stairs?'

'Yes, over the stairs.'

The two older boys sniggered, and then lifted Baker over the stair railing until the poor lad was hanging over the void above the stairwell. The junior boy looked down and saw that he was now around ten yards above the ground floor far below him. He could see the stairwell winding its way down. If they dropped him now he would fall in between the stairs all the way to the bottom floor below.

'Pull me back,' he cried desperately. 'Please lift me back.'

Hedge had been sitting quietly but suddenly rose to his feet. What the boys were doing to his friend looked dangerous. If they dropped him now he could smash his head on the floor below. He would almost certainly be killed.

'Sit down you.' Hedge rested back on knees as Adcock strode towards him. 'Stay where you are. If you move again, then you'll be next.'

Hedge was torn. On the one hand he really wanted to help his mate, but then again, he definitely didn't want to be hung over the stairway.

'Start shaking him about,' Adcock commanded.

The two seniors were laughing. Both together, they started to move the leg they were holding up and down, and side to side. The effect this had was that Baker's head and body were rotating violently above the void below.

Baker was screaming now. The three senior boys were laughing hysterically. Hedge sat quietly watching, afraid to do anything to help.

Then suddenly, one of the senior boys lost his grip on the leg he was holding. He reached out to try and recover his hold on it, but all he succeeded in doing was ripping off one of the lad's shoes. Baker shrieked in panic. The other senior boy tried desperately to hold on to the weight of the boy, but it was too much, and then he too lost his hold.

Baker's leg slipped from his grasp and the boy dropped. Luckily, as the hold on the first leg was lost, the boy was swinging towards one side of the stairwell. This meant that instead of dropping down the void in the middle of the stairs, Baker only fell to the next landing down. Even so, it was a distance of three or four yards, and he landed with a thump on the hard floor below.

There was a loud crash as the boys head hit the ground, followed by a sharp crack, like a branch snapping on a dead tree. Baker's left arm had fallen behind his body and broke clean in two as it landed at an awkward angle.

Adcock was laughing his head off. 'That was hilarious.' He leaned over the railing to look down at Baker lying on the floor below. 'I hope you haven't damaged any school property down there.'

Hedge had regained his bravery. 'You're a fucking dickhead,' he shouted at Adcock as he ran past him and down the stairs.

The other senior boys looked a bit shocked. 'Let's get out of here,' one of them said. They ran off, followed closely behind by Adcock.

Hedge checked that Baker was still breathing. He was, but he was crying out in pain, and sobbing uncontrollably. 'I'll go and get help,' he said and ran off downstairs.

Baker was lucky to survive. But he suffered a broken arm, a fractured collar bone, two broken ribs, and a minor head injury. No action was taken against the senior boys as the two juniors were reluctant to tell the housemaster exactly what happened.

'I think Baker slipped and fell over the railing by accident,' Hedge lied to him.

'You're lucky that I don't punish you both for messing about,' the housemaster had replied.

'We are lucky indeed.' Hedge tried to disguise the sarcasm in his voice.

Chapter Forty

Laura was beginning to feel like a prisoner. She only left her room each day to go and eat meals, and for trips to the bathroom. At all other times she either sat on her bed playing with some toys that Nina had given her, or she watched the small television that was on a table in the corner. The programmes on the TV were rubbish, certainly not like she had back in her real house.

She missed her mother badly, and wondered if she was worried where Laura might be. She still cried quite a lot, especially at night.

The highlight of her day occurred after lunch. There would be a short knock at her door, and then Hala would quietly enter. She was allowed to come and visit but only for a short while. Nina, the Jordanian girl's mother, had told her not to get too tired.

Laura wanted to ask why she would get tired. All they did was play games and talk. Well Hala did, Laura listened. She wondered if maybe Hala was unwell. As soon as her voice returned to normal she would ask her.

After a few days of playing together, they started to become good friends. Laura looked forward to their time together, and she had even started laughing again. Hala was good at making funny faces. Laura giggled when her new friend was being silly.

One such afternoon, they were both jumping about on the bed, pretending it was a trampoline. Hala was trying to touch the roof as she bounced higher, and Laura thought it was hilarious. They were making a lot of noise, but they didn't care. It was great fun.

Suddenly the bedroom door burst open.

'You quiet. Too noisy.' Nina looked angry. She walked over and took hold of Hala's hand. 'Come now. It's time.'

Hala tried to protest, but Nina just slapped her around the leg, and pulled the young girl towards the door. She was shouting at her daughter in a strange language. It didn't make any sense to Laura, although the woman sounded annoyed.

'I want to stay with you Laura.' But then Hala disappeared and the door banged shut.

Laura was worried. Where were they taking her? What did the mother mean by 'It's time?' Hala looked unhappy. Were they going to hurt her?

She decided to try and follow them. If Hala was in some kind of trouble, then maybe she would need help. Laura opened the door carefully, and headed along the corridor in the direction of the noise. She went down one flight of stairs, and then another. She could hear Hala still pleading with her mother.

It was dark at the bottom of the stairs, and a fair bit colder. The others had disappeared now, and Laura couldn't work out where they had gone. She walked slowly down the corridor, feeling her hands along the stone wall. Then, a little way further on, was a white painted door, and bright light was coming from a gap at the bottom of it. She put one of her ears against the door and listened carefully. It sounded like her friend was crying, and her mother was still shouting at her. Very slowly, she pushed on the door, and a small crack appeared between it and the frame. Most of the room was now visible through the gap.

Directly in front of the door, Hala was sitting in a large, plastic covered chair. It looked comfortable, with soft armrests, and a big cushion to rest the head against. Next to this was an enormous machine that looked like it might have come from outer space. It had flashing lights, and wires, and a bleeping screen. Laura thought it looked frightening.

But that wasn't the worst of it. To her astonishment, she watched as a man standing behind Hala started to push a large needle in her friend's arm. Then, he began to connect her up to the machine, and he taped some wires to her arm.

Laura couldn't believe what she was seeing. And then the final horror, the machine started sucking Hala's blood out of her arm. This was surely an alien monster consuming her new best friend. She had to act before it was too late. With a hard shove, she pushed the door open, and burst into the room. Running across to where Hala sat, she tried to grab hold of one of the wires and pull it off the arm it was attached to.

'Leave her alone. Don't you hurt my friend,' she screamed.

Before she could reach any of the other wires, the man had managed to take hold of both her arms. She recognised him as the person she had seen when she'd first arrived at the house, just after she'd been taken out of the crate. As he held her in his grip, she could still smell fish on his breath, just like she had done before.

Now the man was laughing, and then suddenly the mother was laughing. 'We not hurt her. Do not be silly.'

And then Hala was laughing too. 'It's okay Laura. Don't worry I'm fine.'

Laura stopped struggling. She looked towards the big, white-panelled machine. 'I thought that monster was sucking out your blood?'

The Jordanian girl laughed even louder.

'It's not a monster. It's my friend.'

'I'm sorry. I thought ...'

'Don't worry about it.' She smiled across at Laura.

'And I'm really glad you can finally talk.'

Chapter Forty One

Hala's father's name was Khalid. Laura thought he had a kind looking face, and when he spoke it was in a soft, friendly tone. Quite different to when she'd first met him. He had taken her back to her bedroom, while Hala had been reconnected to the machine.

He spoke good English, and started to chat to Laura about how she was feeling, and if she was being well looked after. It was quite a relief that she could now speak properly again. She had worried that the loss of her voice would be forever.

Khalid explained that it was the stress that she had been under recently. Strange things often happen to people when they are worried about things, or have had a bad experience.

She had certainly had that, she thought to herself.

Laura explained that she was feeling unhappy and really wanted to return home. The man just nodded back at her, but didn't actually comment on what she had just said. Instead he started to talk about his daughter.

'Hala is ill, and has to spend some time each day having kidney dialysis. Do you know what that is?'

Laura shook her head. It didn't sound like much fun.

'She has a problem with parts of her body called the kidneys. These are clever gadgets that clean the blood in your body.'

'Why does blood get dirty?' Laura looked puzzled.

Khalid laughed. 'It's hard to explain, but has anyone ever told you not to put too much salt on your food?'

Laura nodded. 'Yes, sometimes.'

'Well, if you eat too much salt, it builds up in the blood that goes around your body. That's not good, and you could become unwell. So the kidneys help to remove things like salt from your blood and so keep you healthy. Do you see what I mean?'

Laura nodded. That made sense.

'Hala's kidneys don't work properly, so if we didn't help her then she would become very sick. The machine you saw downstairs is a big cleaning machine. It takes out some of her blood every day, removes the horrible things, and then puts it back in her body.'

'That's clever,' said Laura. 'Does she have to connect to the machine every day?

'Yes, unfortunately, she needs to spend maybe one hour every day having her blood refreshed.'

Laura looked thoughtful for a while.

'Will she die?' she said bluntly.

'Yes, eventually. But the regular dialysis helps for now.'

She felt sad for her new friend, but Laura was also unhappy herself. 'Why am I here? When can I go back to my proper mummy?'

Khalid was silent for am moment. He looked uncomfortable. When he eventually spoke, she thought he looked a little tearful.

'We really need to give Hala as much happiness as we can, before she ... well, before ...'

'Before she dies?'

He nodded. There was another silence and then he continued. 'I wanted her to have a special friend, to help her to have fun, to lift her spirits, even if it's just for a little while.'

Laura looked confused. It was a lot for her young mind to take in. She sensed that she was being given some great responsibility, but she wasn't sure that was quite fair. She was only a little girl. But Hala was her friend now. She had to help. Even so, she desperately missed her real home, and her real mother.

She stared at the man. 'And after that I can go home?'

Khalid looked at her and nodded.

Chapter Forty Two

The Jordanian National bank building was located in the main business district of the city. It was a hot day, the sun was fierce overhead, and there was virtually no wind. But, regardless of the heat, Hedge and Cole decided to walk the mile and a half from their hotel to the bank. It would be a good way of getting their bearings around the capital.

'I'm sweating like a pig.' Hedge complained as they arrived at the bank. There were small damp patches dotted across the front of his shirt.

'Someone once told me that pigs don't actually sweat.' Cole looked smug, 'Although, I have no idea if that's true or not.'

'Whatever,' replied Hedge, 'I'm still bloody hot.'

They were now standing in front of a large, imposing, stone building. It stretched up four storeys high, and had a striking, polished metal door at the front.

The dark-skinned man on the reception desk looked at the letter that Cole produced, and then picked up his handset and called the manager. After a brief conversation on the phone, he turned back to Cole.

'Mr. Hourani will be with you in a few moments. Please take a seat.'

The manager arrived about ten minutes later, apologised for the delay and ushered them into a smartly decorated meeting room. Cole showed him the letter of introduction he had been given at the British embassy.

'Ah yes, Mr Wilkinson, he is such a fine fellow.' Hourani spoke with a precise manner. His hands shook slightly as he held the letter. Hedge noticed. He always picked up these sorts of habits in other people. Stress maybe, he thought. It must be a high pressure job being head of such an operation as this.

'So what can I do for you two gentlemen?'

Cole explained that they were working indirectly for the British government, and that they were trying to follow up some leads on a human trafficking gang. Some of the payments made to the group had come from this bank. Cole handed the manager a photocopied sheet showing several bank transactions.

'I was hoping you could give us the name and address of the account owners who made these payments.'

Hourani looked quite distressed. 'I can assure you that none of our customers are involved in illegal activities. That would be most improper. We have strict security guidelines and procedures in relation to our account holders.'

'Nevertheless,' Cole tried to keep his tone polite, 'Perhaps you may be able to give us some contact details so that we could follow these up for ourselves.'

Again, the distressed look appeared. 'Giving out customer details is certainly not allowed, and actually is quite illegal in our country. I'm afraid I cannot help you.'

Cole pushed the photocopied page closer to Hourani. 'Please. It could help to recover children who have been abducted. It's important.'

Hourani pushed the sheet back towards Cole. 'Like I say, it's impossible that any of our clients are involved. I cannot help you.' He stole a quick look at his watch. 'I must go now as I have further appointments.'

The manger stood and opened the door. He held it as his two visitors filed out. Once back outside Cole ripped up the letter he had been given by Wilkinson and dropped it into a nearby rubbish bin.

'That was a waste of bloody time.'

Hedge nodded. 'Perhaps we should get a lift back to the hotel. I'm not sure my shirt could stand any more sweat soaking into it.'

Cole laughed, and shouted down an old Mercedes that was driving slowly past. It had a yellow taxi light on its roof.

'Good idea,' he replied to Hedge. 'Screw this fucking heat.'

After a short journey, they arrived back at the hotel. They took a couple of seats in the restaurant and ordered some lunch. Cole's steak sandwich arrived first, followed by Hedge's goat cheese salad.

'I don't know how you can eat that shit.'

Hedge feigned a shocked reaction. 'Are you serious, this is as healthy as it gets. You might not look as old as you do if you'd had more of this stuff in the past.'

Cole sniggered. 'That Hourani was an idiot, don't you think.'

Hedge shrugged. 'Just doing his job I guess. What next then?'

Cole took another bite of his lunch and chewed for a while. Then he produced a small slip of paper from his shirt pocket. Hedge craned his head to look. It appeared to be a list of times and dates.

'What's that?'

I asked an intelligence contact in London to send me a list of all unscheduled flights to Amman in the last two weeks.

'Why just flights, I thought our bad guys were using boats to transport their cargo?' Hedge felt a bit sick inside. He didn't mean cargo. He just didn't want to call them children.

'Yes that's true. And that's okay for the first leg from Florida to Cuba. But I'm guessing they would then finish the journey to Jordan on a plane. Travelling by sea would take way too long.'

Hedge nodded in agreement. He then pointed towards the slip of paper.

So how many inbound flights have there been?

'In the last fourteen days, just over two hundred.'

'Great. So that will be easy to sift through.' Hedge's voice was loaded with sarcasm.

Cole laughed. 'Luckily for us though, only two of them began their journey in Cuba.'

Chapter Forty Three

The manager in charge of the Amman International Airport Authority was not an easy person to arrange to see. It had been relatively straightforward getting into the administration building at the airport, but securing an appointment with the very busy Mr Badawi was proving difficult.

Cole was losing his temper with the unflinching man at the reception desk.

'Tell him that we are on important government business.'

'I keep advising you, Mr. Badawi is tied up all day. Please return tomorrow and I will see what I can do for you.'

Cole had no intention of coming back tomorrow. 'How about I just punch you and as you lie unconscious on the floor, we walk past and find the manager ourselves?'

The man looked horrified. He was about to reach for an alarm button on the side of his desk.

Hedge stepped in close to him. 'Don't do that. Please ignore my friend here. I have a better proposition for you.'

He reached into his jacket pocket and pulled out a bundle of notes. The cash should have been used to pay for the weapons, but as it turned out they had acquired them for free. Slowly counting out roughly two hundred dollars worth of the local currency, he then laid the small pile on the desk. Hedge looked up at the man and smiled.

'Do you think Mr. Badawi is available yet?'

The man stared at Hedge for a brief moment. Then he scooped up the pile of notes and shoved them into his trouser pocket. 'I will go and check for you.'

Two hours later they were back at their hotel in the centre of the capital. The meeting with Badawi had gone well. It turned out that the man had been in the Jordanian military before he had taken up his present employment. The highlight of his time in the army had been when his unit had joined a large exercise organised by the Saudi Arabians. British Special Forces had also been involved, and so he and Cole had reminisced about how much fun they had both had in the Arabian Desert back then.

'Were you really there?' Hedge had enquired on the drive back to Amman. 'And surely you didn't really remember that Badawi guy?'

'Yes, I was there. And no, I don't remember him at all. There were two thousand Arab troops. But he seemed delighted when I said I recognised him. It would have been a shame to spoil that by telling the truth.'

Hedge laughed. 'Well we got what we wanted.'

That was true enough. The man had been most obliging. Of the two landings they were investigating, one could be eliminated immediately as Badawi had said it was a military cargo shipment. He had personally gone on board that aircraft as a guest of a senior ranking army officer. Badawi couldn't comment further, but he hoped they would trust him when he said it was not what they were looking for.

Cole was pretty good with weighing people up. He completely trusted the man.

The second cargo plane was an unusual one. It wasn't a regular flight into Amman. Badawi remembered it well, as there weren't many older-style, ex-military cargo planes in operation in this part of the world. And the Russian Antonov was very distinctive.

They now had the address of the company that handled that flight.

'We need to go and pay them a visit, don't you think?' It was more of a statement from Cole than a question.

Hedge suddenly became very nervous. Somehow he sensed that a more dangerous part of the mission was about to begin. He started to feel a bit hot, so he moved the vehicle's air-conditioning dial to a slightly cooler setting. But the control knob didn't look right. He preferred it when it either pointed straight up or straight down. A setting exactly in the middle of this was also acceptable. But the knob was pointing to roughly the ten o'clock position. That didn't feel right. He moved it down a fraction and left it at nine o'clock. That position was fine, albeit the car's temperature was now a little too cool.

'Stop pissing about with that.' Cole was concentrating on driving, but had noticed his friend's anxious behaviour. 'Playing with that isn't going to make what we have to do next any easier.'

Hedge was slightly embarrassed. 'I'm not playing. I'm just trying to get the heating right. Anyway, what have we got to do next that's so terrible?'

'I'm not sure,' replied Cole, 'but we need to stop by the hotel and pick up the two G30's. And I hope the package that I requested from Wilkinson has been delivered. We're going to need that.'

'What is it?'

'You'll find out. I suspect that we may come across someone who is not too keen to tell us what we want to know. They may need some encouragement.'

Hedge felt a sickening feeling in the pit of his stomach.

Reaching forward, he turned the air-conditioning knob down to the six o'clock position. It looked a bit tidier like that.

But he still felt sick.

Chapter Forty Four

Hedge waited in the car while Cole scurried into the hotel to collect the things they needed. Ten minutes late he was back. He flicked open the storage compartment in front of the passenger seat and placed the two handguns inside. Then he pulled out a small, glass bottle, and gently laid that next to the G30's.

Hedge looked at the items nervously. Cole said nothing as he started the engine and drove off.

'Have you still got the address?'

Cole nodded.

Hedge sat quietly for a while, lost in his own thoughts. Cole was also quiet. He drove slowly, in silence and looking slightly subdued.

'Are you thinking about the girl?'

Cole nodded again. 'Yes maybe, and some other things.'

'Are you getting a bit sentimental in your old age?'

'Yeah right, perhaps I'll turn into a worried little boy like you.'

'You're not as tough as you think Cole.'

It was banter, friendly goading between the two of them. But underneath it all, there were some hidden truths.

They sat quietly again for a moment. Then Hedge turned to his friend. The question came out of nowhere. 'What's the worst thing you have ever done then?'

Cole thought for a while. 'Are you sure you want to know?'

'Are you sure you want to tell?'

Cole shook his head, and smiled softly. His eyes stared unblinking at the road ahead. Then he began to tell the story.

He had been assigned from his regular army unit to a special operation, working alongside members of the British Parachute Regiment in the small West African country of Sierra Leone. The year was 2000, and a civil war was raging. A small naval flotilla from the UK had arrived off the coast and landed some fifteen hundred troops. Their objective was to oppose the rebel army approaching the capital city, Freetown.

There was a short battle outside Lungi airport and the rebels were defeated. The intervention by the British army was totally successful, helping to bring peace to the country.

Hedge had been listening with interest. 'Sounds all good to me so far, so where was the problem?'

Cole ignored him and carried on. He was still staring directly ahead. His voice softened slightly.

'I wasn't actually involved in the fighting. It seemed they wanted my Special Forces intelligence gathering skills. The village where I had set up my base was quite a long way from the front line. It was supposed to be safe. So we were told anyway. But, early one morning, around five thirty, we were attacked by a group of rebel soldiers. It seemed like they came out of nowhere. They were heavily armed, Russian weapons mainly, but poorly trained and organised. There were only six of us in our group, but we were professionals. We killed all seventeen of the attackers, with only a single minor injury to one of our group.'

Hedge nodded. 'Impressive.'

Cole ignored the slightly mocking praise.

'So it was all over in a few minutes. No serious harm done to any of our men. I called the situation in to HQ and they told us to evacuate the base immediately. The threat of further attacks was likely. I told them that we hadn't quite finished our work. Another day or so would do it. But the commanding officer insisted. So we packed up and started moving out. I was the last man to leave. I wanted to make sure we hadn't left anything behind. We had a lot of sensitive gear with us. Just as I was climbing aboard the truck, I saw a figure run out of the bush near me. It was a man, holding a gun, and it was pointing directly at me. The look on his face was terrifying. Without thinking, I levelled my weapon and fired a short burst towards the figure. The upper part of his head disintegrated and he fell down dead.'

'So, it was a lucky escape for you. I can understand how that would be pretty scary.'

Cole smiled. But it was an uncomfortable smile.

'That wasn't the scary bit. Plenty of people have tried to shoot me, and failed. No. It was when I went across to search the body that I suddenly realised that this was no man. It was a boy. With such a large part of his face missing, it was hard to tell his age. That was until I found his school notepad in his trouser pocket. The heading on the front read "Name – Kossi" followed by "Age – 5". I searched the undergrowth nearby for the lad's weapon. I couldn't find it. All I found was a short bamboo stick that had been painted black, and a bag of marbles.'

'Bloody hell,' Hedge had turned white. The mocking joviality had left his voice. 'The poor kid, what happened to the body, did you take it with you, or bury him?'

Cole turned and looked at his friend. 'We had no choice. We had to leave him where he lay. We left him to the wild animals.' Then his voice trailed off.

Hedge stared out of the window.

He wished he'd never asked the question.

Chapter Forty Five

The warehouse in front of them looked deserted. It was an old structure, badly maintained, and a long way from anywhere. They had driven several miles north of Amman and turned off onto a dusty track, shortly after passing through a small village.

'Are you sure this is the place?' Hedge climbed out of the car to get a better look.

Cole nodded. 'This is it. We have followed Badawi's directions to the letter. It doesn't look like much is happening here.'

Hedge didn't answer. The building gave him the creeps. There was a half open door just in front of him. He walked slowly over to it, poked his head through the gap, and quickly withdrew it.

'Did you hear that? It sounds like the place is haunted or something.'

Hedge had backed away from the entrance. His face had turned pale. Cole pushed past him and stepped inside the dark opening. Laughing softly, he walked back out into the sunlight. As he did so he pulled the Glock G30 from his belt, and checked that it was loaded.

'That's no ghost you heard. Don't you know what that is?'

Hedge shook his head. He didn't trust his voice to reply.

Cole frowned at him. 'Follow me, but do it quietly. I'll show you what I think we have stumbled across.'

He led the way into the building. It was dark, but their eyes soon became accustomed to the gloom. They walked past an old forklift truck, several stacks of cardboard packaging, and a few large, wooden crates. One of the crates had its top open, and Cole held up his hand and pointed across to it. The two of them headed

158

over to look at it, but quickly backed away when they suddenly became aware of the foul smell coming from inside it.

'It smells like somebody had died in there, or at best they must have shit themselves badly.'

Hedge didn't reply. The odour had made him feel sick. He wanted to vomit, but held it back. It was the sort of thing that Cole would have loved to see him do. He would have gleaned amusement from it for years to come.

There was the noise again. It was a soft moaning, like somebody nearby was being slowly tortured. Now there was a sharp scream, followed by a loud grunt. It was definitely a human noise. Hedge couldn't bear to listen. He suspected that they were going to find a horribly mutilated body.

Cole held his G30 in his right hand, and motioned them forwards. Just ahead was a closed door. Holding the gun up high in front of him, he kicked his right foot hard towards the door handle. The lock gave way under the impact and the door flew open. Cole stepped into the room, closely followed by Hedge. There was a low hanging ceiling light in the middle of the room, so they could clearly see what was happening in front of them.

There was no ghost.

In front of them were real people, two of them, and both were completely naked. The woman had been leaning forward over a waist-high table. She had ceased her gentle moaning noises as soon as she heard the crash of the door. Her eyes were now wide open in disbelief, and she had lifted the front of her body up from the table. As she did so, her breasts bounced underneath her. The first thing that Cole noticed was her strikingly pale face with her hard-set jaw line.

The man standing behind her was tall and Arabic-looking. He had a dark, well-groomed beard, but that didn't completely cover the shock that was now showing on his face. It had taken a couple of seconds after the door had caved in for him to stop his rhythmic pounding into the woman. Had he not have been so close to his climax, he would have ceased much quicker.

As it was, the moment had gone. He was both annoyed and shocked by the sudden intrusion. Before even extracting himself from his partner, he reached for the pistol that was lying on the table. He managed to grab it, click off the safety catch, and almost pull it round towards where Cole was standing, before the bullet from the G30 passed through one side of his head and out of the other.

The Arab slumped down on top of the woman. Blood was pouring out of the huge exit wound on the far side of his skull. The red liquid, mixed up with small pieces of bone and brain tissue, had started to run down the woman's back.

She screamed while desperately trying to push the dead man off her. Cole had taken several quick steps towards her, and with the gun still in his right hand, was forcing her head down hard onto the table.

'You and I are going to have a little chat, my girl. Are you ready for that, or do you want to get yourself cleaned up first.'

'Fuck you.' She tried to push her head up off the table, but Cole held it firm.

'Or fuck you, don't you mean. It looks like your dead friend here is still trying to satisfy you.' Cole laughed out loud.

To her horror, the woman realised that the dead man was still inside her. She shouted out, struggling to get up as she did so. Cole released his grip on her with his left hand, and as her head came up, he smashed the butt of the G30 hard against her temple. Her head dropped back onto the table. She was out cold.

Hedge had been watching the scene in disbelief. There was blood all over the woman. 'Now what do we do?'

'Well I'm going to get rid of this guy.' Cole pulled the dead man off the back of the woman, and started to drag him away. 'And you are going to sort out our blonde haired friend here. Find something to secure her with, and then tie her to one of those chairs. I'll be back in a moment.' He carried on hauling the dead body out of the room.

'Do you want me to find her some clothes?' Hedge shouted after him.

'No. I wouldn't bother.'

Chapter Forty Six

Olga was starting to stir. She had a massive headache, and was finding it difficult to focus her eyes. Her hands and feet had been tightly bound to the metal chair that she was now sitting on. The air in the room was slightly damp, and she felt cold. In front of her were two men. They seemed to be discussing a container that one of them was holding in his hands.

'Where did that come from?' Hedge was asking.

Cole looked pleased with himself. 'I predicted this moment would arrive. This is what I requested our embassy friend to get hold of.'

'What is it?' Hedge tried to grab the glass bottle.

'Don't touch. This is precious stuff.'

'What is it?' The question was repeated.

'Well chemists call it Sodium Pentothal, but it's often just known as Truth Serum.'

Hedge looked mystified, but remained silent.

'It's called that because it can make certain people become very talkative. Hopefully they will then answer any questions that you ask them.'

Cole took out a thin, glass syringe, with a long needle on the end of it. Carefully, he opened the top of the bottle, dipped the needle into the chemical, and then pulled the plunger on the syringe sucking up some of the clear liquid as he did so. He closed the lid on the glass bottle tight.

Casting his eyes across to his friend, he slowly nodded. Then, with a beaming smile on his face, he walked back towards the woman, pulled up another chair beside hers, and sat down.

161

'I just want to ask you a few questions. We need your help to track down a missing girl.'

Olga tried to stay confident. It was difficult, as she was completely naked and tied securely. She felt vulnerable and afraid. She couldn't stop looking at the long needle in Cole's hand.

'I don't know what you're talking about. I'm just an employee for a freight handling company. We ship seeds and cigars mainly. I really can't help you. Please let me go.'

Cole leaned forward and held up the syringe. 'This won't hurt too much, you'll just feel a small prick under your skin, and then you'll start to relax.' He hesitated for a moment as if he was thinking, then he continued. 'By the way, the only known side effects, apart from drowsiness, are permanent loss of memory, and occasionally sterilisation. So hopefully you haven't got too many good memories, and you don't want to ever have kids.'

'You wouldn't dare. Please, I don't know anything.' The woman's voice had an edge of panic. She looked across towards Hedge, hoping that he was the gentler of the two men. 'Please. You wouldn't let him hurt me.'

Hedge sensed something in the woman. There was hardness about her. Even though her pale, Eastern European complexion gave her a seductive look, she seemed somehow remote, and dangerous.

'He would hurt you. You see we are looking for a six year old girl. She's been stolen from her mother. We think you know something about that. You need to tell us what you know.'

Cole looked up at his friend. It seemed odd and very out of character to hear him talk so boldly. He nodded towards Hedge. It was an acknowledgment of him saying the right thing at the right time. It wasn't often that Cole gave away praise, but that's exactly what he had just done. And he hadn't even said anything.

Cole now turned back to the woman. He moved the syringe towards her upper arm. She screamed at him and tried to pull away. Then, holding her arm in his left hand, he used his right hand to stick the needle hard into her arm. He pushed the plunger fully inside the syringe and the liquid was forced into her bloodstream.

To Hedge, it looked like an immediate change had come over the woman. Initially, it must have been painful as Olga was howling and crying at the same time. She was trying to pull free of her bonds but the rope was holding her securely to the chair. The more she struggled, the further the serum seemed to take hold of her.

A few moments later the woman's head dropped down onto her chest. Her eyes were half-closed and she had started chattering to herself in a soft, quiet voice.

'Is it working?' Hedge had suddenly become interested. He had never seen a drug used before to try and get information from someone.

'It will soon. Normally the victim begins to talk incessantly. The trick is to get them onto the subject that's important to you.'

Cole pulled his chair nearer to the woman's. He leaned close to her to make sure she could hear him above the sound of her own chatting and sobbing.

'Now tell me about the girl, the young girl, the one you people stole from her mother.'

Olga looked up at him. A smile spread across her face. She looked drunk, and her eyes seemed unable to focus. When she spoke her voice was slurred and unclear.

'Yes, young girl. I like girls. But don't tell anyone. It's a sheecret.' As she tried to say the last word it came out rather slurred.

'What's a secret?' Cole pushed her on that.

'You know, that I like girls. I just told you. Didn't you listen? You're a dumb man. I just told you.'

'And what do you do with girls?'

The woman giggled. 'That's a stupid question. We play together of course.' This followed by more giggling. 'We undress, and touch each other, all over, and inside. Yes, I love girls. But don't tell my mother.'

'So where is Laura? Did you touch her?'

Olga whipped her head round to stare at Cole. 'That's disgusting. She's too young. I don't like little girls, too young. You're a pervert.'

Hedge laughed. He could see Cole getting angry. The woman was taking him round in circles. 'I think she's trying to tell you that she's a lesbian. But it's a sheecret.'

'Didn't look like that ten minutes ago,' Cole sneered.

Now it was Olga's turn to laugh. Then she was speaking again, still in a slurred, almost drunk-like voice. 'That was fun, but not as nice as another woman. Actually, I'm glad you killed him, he was horrible.'

'What about Laura?'

'I don't know ....'

Olga's voice trailed off as Cole slapped her hard around the face. The blow snapped her head back, and then she began to cry again. The woman looked pathetic. Sitting tied to the chair, naked, and sobbing like a child.

Cole put his face hard up against hers. 'Tell me about the little girl.'

'I didn't hurt her, just dropped her off. She seemed okay the last time I saw her. Yes, definitely okay. Such a young one, but it's my job, you know. She was okay. I think anyway. But okay. We took her to the place. They were expecting her.'

The woman was rambling. Cole needed specifics. He raised his arm and slapped her hard once more. Instantly, she stopped talking and looked at him. There was fear in her face, but also anger, and a little confusion.

As she watched him, he opened the glass bottle again and filled up the syringe once more. Turning his hand round so that she could see it, he held up the needle while he studied Olga's naked body.

'They say the second injection is much more painful.'

He carried on looking her up and down. Suddenly a devious smile spread across his face. He reached out with his free hand, and gently cupped her right breast. Pulling his hand upwards slowly, he ran his finger over her nipple.

'Okay, so the breast it is.'

He moved the syringe towards its target. She flinched, and tried to pull away, but couldn't. The needle was now just an inch away from the soft, white skin at the top of her bosom. Olga was shaking her head from side to side, screaming and shouting incoherently.

Suddenly her words became meaningful. The needle was almost touching her skin.

'Her name is Laura. The girl is called Laura. Please, don't hurt me, I'll tell you what I know.' The woman had suddenly become more coherent. It was as if she had awoken from a slumber. Her eyes sparkled brightly, and she seemed much more focused on her situation.

Cole pulled his arm away from her. For several minutes he asked her questions and she answered them, sometimes coherently, sometimes not. Finally, when he was satisfied that they had all they needed, he pulled out his Glock.

The woman looked shocked. 'I've told you all I know. Please, let me go.'

'I made a promise to the girl's mother.' Cole had a serious look on his face.

Hedge took a step forward and touched his forearm. 'Leave her. She's not important.'

Cole looked at his friend. They held each other's eyes for a moment. Then he nodded, and pushed the pistol back into his pocket. They left the woman tied to the chair and walked back outside to where they had parked the car. Cole jumped into the driver's seat, but Hedge was busy making a call on his cell phone. When he had finished he too got into the vehicle.

Cole hesitated before he pulled away. 'I still don't think that bitch should get away without any punishment.'

Hedge laughed. 'And that is why I have just called the office of the main religious daily newspaper in Amman'

'And told them what exactly?'

'That there's a naked white woman at this address offering free sex to all Arab men who come along today.'

'She'll get a public flogging for that.' Cole chuckled.

'Fifty lashes I expect.'

'At least that,' Cole replied as he throttled the car, 'maybe even a hundred.'

Chapter Forty Seven

'This is the address that the woman gave us.' Cole stopped the car on the side of a narrow road.

They had driven close to twenty miles since leaving the old warehouse. Entering Amman from the north east, their route had taken them along Army Street, before they had pulled onto a wide road known as Ash Shahid. This had turned them in a westerly direction for a few miles, before circling around the Prince Hashem Bird Garden.

The traffic on their journey had been relatively light for a change. Hedge had been sitting quietly, studying the buildings and monuments as they passed by. Finally they had entered a wealthy looking neighbourhood on the western outskirts of the city.

'It's a nice looking place,' Hedge commented.

The house in front of them was large by Amman standards. It was constructed of square, off-white stone, with lots of brown, shuttered windows dotted on each level. The front porch had a large cast-iron gate set into it, and in front of this was a row of bay trees in decorative, wooden pots.

Cole was already climbing out of the car. 'Let's go and introduce ourselves.'

Hedge swallowed hard when he saw the G30 sticking out of the back of Cole's trousers. Even though he had been told to bring his own, he ignored the request and left it lying in the front storage compartment.

Striding quickly towards the front of the house, Cole had already reached the gates and was pulling them open. He waited for

Hedge to catch up, and then he banged hard on the heavy-looking front door.

The man who opened the door was small. He had short, black hair and a well trimmed, dark moustache. He looked like he was about to say something, but it was too late. Cole had grabbed the man by his throat, lifting him off his feet at the same time. Still holding the man, he strode into the hallway of the house, and beckoned Hedge to follow. Then he kicked the door shut.

'Who are you, and who else is home at the moment?'

It was difficult for the man to speak as it felt like he was being strangled. His face had turned a deep red colour, and his arms were waving frantically in the air.

Hedge took a step forwards as he spoke. 'If you don't let him go, he won't be telling you anything. Another thirty seconds and he'll be dead. Let him go you big ape.'

Cole grunted, and dropped the man onto the ground. With his foot resting on the man's neck, he pushed his head onto the hard, marble flooring. The Glock was now in his right hand and he rested the dangerous end of it on the small man's nose.

'Who are you?'

The man was panic-stricken. He could see the danger in Cole's eyes, and he could feel the cold of the pistol on his face.

'My name is Adama. I am the housekeeper. I look after the house for Mr Khalid and his family.'

Hedge looked surprised. 'Housekeeper, I thought that was normally a female's job?'

'Not here in Jordan. Mainly men, like me.' Adama was struggling to speak. His head was still being pressed against the hard surface of the floor.

Cole seemed annoyed. 'I don't give a shit about who does what.' He pushed the end of the G30 hard against Adama's face. 'What I want to know is who else lives in this house?'

'It's Mr. Khalid and his wife, their daughter, and I. And occasionally the cook stays here, but not all the time.'

'Is there anyone else?'

'No, that's it. There's nobody else.'

'Are there any other children in the house?' The gun was still pressing against the man's face. Such was the force of it that blood had started to seep from a small wound where the end of the barrel had dug into Adama's skin.

The man went quiet. He looked uncomfortable. It had suddenly occurred to him that there was a young girl staying with them at the moment. Khalid had told him to say nothing about her to anyone. He had been quite specific about that. If word got out about the new visitor then Adama would be fired from his job. It was a dilemma. Then he caught the eyes of the man staring down at him from above, and he felt the trickle of blood running along his own face. He made his decision.

'Yes, a little girl, a friend of Khalid's daughter. She is visiting us at the moment.'

'Where is she?'

'They have all gone to the hospital. The daughter is very sick and has some treatment arranged. The address is on the card over there on that table. It's the appointment letter in the white envelope.'

'How long have they been gone?'

'They left about one hour ago, or maybe a little more.'

Cole took his foot off the man's head. As he stepped back he raised the Glock until it was pointing at the figure still lying on the floor.

Hedge took a pace forward. 'Cole, no don't.'

'I made a promise to the girl's mother.'

Hedge took another pace forward, effectively putting himself between the gun and Adama.

'No. Leave him.'

Cole lowered his arm and then stuffed the G30 back into his trousers. He walked to the table and picked up the white envelope. As he started to read the letter inside, his face turned pale.

'Fucking hell, we need to get going, right now.'

Chapter Forty Eight

'Where are we all going?' Laura asked.

It was the first time she'd been out of the house since she'd arrived in this strange place. She was sitting in the back of a large car. Next to her sat Hala. In the front were Khalid and Nana, the girl's mother and father.

'Today is a special day for Hala.' Khalid's voice sounded slightly nervous. He was trying to focus on driving at the same time as answering Laura's question. It wasn't easy, as the traffic at this time of day was quite heavy, and he had a lot on his mind. He turned his head slightly towards the rear of the vehicle as he continued.

'Our daughter is going to the hospital. We have arranged for her to see a specialist doctor. If she is lucky, we may be able to make her well. We are hoping that after seeing this man, her kidneys will work again.'

'Does that mean she won't have to use the big machine ever again?' Laura thought that would be wonderful if so.

'Yes, we hope so.' Khalid glanced briefly across towards Hala's mother. His voice still sounded fearful.

Hala was sitting quietly alongside her new friend. She was clearly worried about what might lie ahead of her today. She hated going to see doctors. It felt like most of her short life had been spent in and out of hospitals, having tests, and being connected to machines. It was all very stressful. If only she could have been like other girls. Some of her friends couldn't remember ever going to see a doctor. Perhaps their father's couldn't afford it, she thought. Or more likely, they didn't have the sort of problems she had to deal with.

Laura took hold of Hala's hand. It felt hot and sweaty, but she held on to it anyway. 'I'll come with you if you like. Things are never as bad when you have a friend with you.'

Hala smiled at her. She gripped Laura's hand tightly, before turning back to face the window. Still she kept quiet, just watching the white-painted, flat-roofed buildings go by outside.

She hated going to hospitals.

It was almost two hours later that a metal framed trolley was wheeled into the operating theatre at a private medical centre on the outskirts of Amman. The young girl lying on the trolley was fast asleep. Hardly surprising really, as just a few seconds ago the anaesthetist had pushed a needle into her arm and injected enough anaesthetic into her bloodstream to keep her knocked out for at least ninety minutes. That would be more than enough time for the operation.

Hala's parents followed the trolley as it headed towards the theatre. They both had concerned looks on their faces. This operation could mean a new way of life for their daughter. The transplant that she would receive would put an end to the daily ritual of being connected up to that awful machine. Hala would be able to go out and play like normal girls her age. It was all too much to hope for. They silently prayed that everything would go well. They had waited for this day for such a long time. It was going to cost them a lot of money, but it would be worth it.

The door to the operating theatre opened, and a tall man dressed in a long, green medical gown stood in the doorway.

'I'll take her from here,' he said. 'Please don't worry. She is in safe hands now. If you take a seat in the waiting room I will come and talk to you in a while, when the process is complete.'

Khalid nodded towards the surgeon and, taking hold of his wife's arm, he walked off towards the waiting area.

Inside the theatre the atmosphere was tense. The doctor pulled on a clean pair of surgical gloves, but it was difficult to disguise his uneasiness. He had performed this kind of operation many times before, so he knew exactly what he was doing. But this one was different. It wasn't the money, although he appreciated the substantial payment he was receiving. The cash would pay for most of his children's university fees, and so it was very welcome. No, it was the nature of what he was doing.

He tried to put his misgivings to one side and focus on the task.

'Scalpel please,' he said holding out his right hand.

The young girl on the operating table lay quite still. Her breathing was slow but regular. The instruments behind her indicated that so far everything was fine.

The man ran a finger on his left hand along the black line marked on the side of the girl's stomach, just above where her kidney was. Then, after just a moment's hesitation, he ran the sharp blade of the scalpel along the same line.

The cut was deep, about one inch into the skin and flesh. The girl's blood started to flow from the wound, but was quickly mopped up by the nurse standing on the other side of the operating table.

Slowly and methodically the surgeon worked to open up the girl's body tissues. Then, finally, he was ready. As if to reassure himself one last time, he leaned forward and read again the small rows of numbers and letters tattooed at the top of the girl's arm. The RBC and WBC numbers related to the red and white blood count. They were good matches.

Satisfied, he turned back to the girl's stomach area, took a tight grip on the scalpel, and moved his hand in closer in order to remove Laura's kidney.

Chapter Forty Nine

The doctor was desperately trying to concentrate, but it wasn't easy. The operation to remove the girl's kidney wasn't a simple one. It needed his full attention, and a steady hand. But he was anxious. Something was gnawing away at him. He was getting paid well for this, very well. But that didn't make it right. And if he was discovered, if he was caught doing this procedure, the consequences would be dire.

He would probably be able to bribe his way out of trouble, but he would lose all the money he had made from the job. However, if his bribes were refused, then he could be prosecuted. It would mean prison, and losing his medical licence. His family would be disgraced.

There was something else that was playing on his mind. Once her kidney had been removed, there was a small chance that the young girl on the table in front of him could have some kind of complication. The procedure was relatively safe, but problems were occasionally encountered.

It was some time ago that he had been approached and asked if he would be interested in carrying out the two operations. The first was the removal process, and the second would be to replace the kidney in the receiving patient. He had been advised that both of the patients involved were young girls, and he'd been assured that the kidney donor was a good match for the recipient. Apparently, it had proven very difficult to find a compatible donor for various reasons, but after extensive blood testing, tissue-typing, and cross-matching, the right candidate had been discovered. Therefore, the likelihood of organ rejection was minimal.

At the time he had specifically asked where the donor organs were coming from. His contact had assured him that they were planning to utilise a girl who was already in an irreversible coma following a serious accident, and the family had agreed to the donation. It was all ethical and properly authorised.

The doctor was no idiot. He now realised that wasn't the case. The young girl in front of him appeared to be perfectly healthy, even though he had only first seen her after she had been anaesthetised.

He directed a few terse words towards the nurse standing on the opposite side of the operating table. She responded to his request and wiped away the sweat from his forehead with a clean paper towel.

Looking down at the girl lying in front of him, he was unsure if he should proceed. He wished that he'd never got himself involved in this in the first place. But now it wasn't just a case of losing the money he had been promised. No, it was the veiled threats that had been made against his family. The people he had found himself mixed up with were not quite what he had originally thought. Not medical professionals as he had expected, but rather some of them behaved more like businessmen, hard-nosed ones at that.

It was an impossible situation for him. He had no choice. He just hoped that the kidney he transplanted into the Jordanian girl was successful. There was a twenty per cent chance that it would be rejected by her body. It was only after he had agreed to carry out the operations, that it had been explained to him what would happen if the initial kidney transplant failed.

'That's preposterous,' he had said at the time. It was difficult to believe what they were suggesting. 'If we take a second kidney from the foreign girl, then it would be giving her a death sentence.'

He had said categorically that he wouldn't do it. Not the second one. But then there had been more of the veiled threats against his family. His only hope was that it wouldn't come to that. The first kidney transplant must succeed.

All the same, he had mentally prepared himself. Just in case he might be required to ring round a few of the major hospitals in the area and see if they could get the girl onto a life support machine. It was the least that he could do if the situation arose. Then maybe, she could be transported back to her home country, wherever that was, and await a kidney donor herself. He promised himself that he would do all he could to save her. That helped to assuage his guilt a little, but not much. He really hoped that that situation would not arise. Pushing the thought from his mind, he attempted to focus back on what he now had to do.

The incision he had made to open up her side was deep, and a steady flow of blood was trickling out. The nurse was kept busy by wiping the blood away. She looked up at the doctor, wondering why he was delaying. She didn't share his concerns about the procedure as she was also being well paid. She just wanted him to get on with it.

The doctor picked up a fresh, steel scalpel. It had a small, razor sharp tip, ideal for the task of removing the child's organ. He took a deep breath in through his face mask, and slowly moved his hand towards the opening in the girl's body.

The enormous bang came as a complete shock to the doctor, and he felt like he was about to suffer a heart attack. The door to the operating theatre flew wide open, almost coming off its hinges. Two men were pushing their way in. Both were holding handguns out in front of them.

The doctor was in a state of complete panic. A split second earlier all of his attention had been focused on the patient on the table in front of him. Now it seemed like all hell had broken loose. He was already nervous, but that had suddenly turned to pure terror. Without thinking, he raised the hand holding the scalpel and lashed out at the nearest man. He didn't know what he was doing, but he was scared, and he reacted instinctively.

The blade caught Cole on the forearm and sliced through skin, tissue and muscle with ease. The cut was deep, and blood started spraying from the wound in all directions. Cole had been caught completely by surprise. He certainly hadn't expected such a quick reaction from anyone inside the room. He immediately dropped his Glock and tried desperately to cover the gash in his arm with his free hand.

Hedge saw the doctor draw back the scalpel ready to strike again. The man's eyes burned with terror and fright. He looked like a mad person on the rampage. Hedge felt like he had no choice. He raised his Glock, but just couldn't bring himself to pull the trigger. He hesitated momentarily, but then, a split second later, he drew his arm back and threw the handgun with all the force he could muster in the direction of the man in the green coat.

The doctor was about to lunge with the scalpel once more, but held back as he saw the black object hurtling towards him. He tried to duck out the way, but the barrel of the gun caught him directly on the forehead, and he immediately fell to the floor.

Then the hospital security staff arrived. There was a lot of shouting, and Hedge found himself being pushed to the ground. It was all over in a few seconds. The doctor was disarmed, and then he and the nurse were led away.

The man was crying uncontrollably. Hedge looked up at him as he passed by. The wound on his forehead seemed to have been forgotten. He held his hands loosely by his side as the security guard pushed him out of the room. Tears were streaming down his face. He looked broken.

One of the security guys was helping Cole to tie a bandage around his damaged arm. Cole sat on the floor of the operating theatre, covered in his own blood. He looked annoyed more than anything else.

Hedge was feeling very anxious about the whole incident, but quite relieved that he had managed to avoid firing the gun. He hated guns. In fact, he hated any violent encounters. Unlike Cole, it wasn't something that was in his nature.

Cole was still sitting on the floor as Hedge was led out of the room. As he walked by, Cole shot a glance at him. He was shaking his head.

'Remind me to give you a lesson in how to use a pistol. Two hundred years of technology has gone into that thing, and you chuck it like a kid in a playground.'

Hedge tried to ignore the remark, but he couldn't let it go.

'Let me know next time you need me to step in and help you out. You just sit down and take it easy. I'll sort out the bad guys.'

Cole grunted and tried to think of something clever in response. But his mind wasn't functioning properly, his arm hurt like hell, so he quickly gave up. 'Fuck off,' was all he managed to say.

Hedge was chuckling loudly now. As he left the room he turned and shouted behind him. 'We need to get you to a hospital Cole.'

His laughter echoed down the corridor.

Chapter Fifty

Laura was holding on to Hedge's hand very tightly. She had been through a lot during the last few weeks, and because of that she trusted no one. That is apart from the man who now held her. He seemed kind, and had promised her that she would soon see her mother again. And that's exactly what the six year old girl wanted most.

'She'll be waiting for you when the airplane lands.' Hedge tried to sound confident. He just hoped that someone had organised for Ann McCain to be picked up and bought to the airport. That was what they had arranged to happen.

'Is her arm still hurting her?' Laura still hadn't forgotten about the incident on the bus. Her mother had screamed so loudly that day. The memory of it made the little girl quite sad.

'I think the doctor will have sorted that out for her. Anyway, the only thing she will be thinking about is seeing you again. Not long now.' Hedge was going to remind her how a kind doctor had fixed her up after her recent accident. But he thought it best not to bring that up again. Laura couldn't remember much about her trip to the hospital. Hedge had told her she had an accident while out playing, and had managed to cut herself somehow. The little girl had believed him. She was actually quite proud of her injury, and kept recounting all the stitches she had on the side of her stomach.

Laura smiled up at Hedge. She gripped his hand even tighter. They were following the signs to the arrivals hall. The flight from Amman to Miami had been a long one, with a change of aircraft at Frankfurt in Germany. But now they were back in Florida.

177

As it happened Ann McCain had been picked up from her home in an FBI car. The driver was a quiet man, so there had been very little conversation on the journey to Miami International airport. She had sat in the back of the car and tried to hold back her tears. Her emotions were all over the place. It had been such incredible news to hear that her daughter had been found alive, especially as she had almost given up hope. All the expert advice she kept reading was that if a missing person was not found quickly, then they were rarely found at all. It was even worse knowing that Laura had almost certainly been taken abroad.

Yes, she had quickly given up hope, and had sunk into a dark, black world. For the last two weeks she'd felt like her own life was over. Now things were different. Was it really her daughter though? Perhaps they had made a mistake and found another young girl. She tried to think positively, but the doubts kept coming into her head.

And what did they mean when they said she was rescued from a hospital. The operation had been interrupted just in time.

'What operation?' she had screamed back. But no proper answer had been provided.

'You will be briefed in full after you have been reunited with your daughter,' she had been told.

The thought of her daughter having some medical operation was horrific. What had they done to her? Was it something permanent? Was she going to be okay? She turned her head and stared out of the car window. The road was racing past as they overtook other vehicles on the freeway. But her eyes couldn't focus, and her mind kept coming back to her daughter. Then, she could hold herself no longer, and tears started streaming down her cheeks. She sat back in her seat and wiped her face with some paper tissues.

The driver slowed the car as he forked off the road towards the airport. He turned and looked at the woman in the back seat. She was sobbing quietly. He tried to think of something sensitive to say, but he couldn't. So he said nothing and concentrated on driving. There was a lot of traffic around outside the arrivals area. He pulled the car over against the kerbside, braked hard to miss a runaway luggage trolley, and then parked the vehicle. He opened the back door to let the woman out, and was relieved to see the airport manager arriving to greet them as had been arranged. The woman was his responsibility now, so the FBI man said goodbye and then quickly drove off back to his office.

As they approached the arrivals area Hedge could see a crowd had gathered to greet many of the passengers. He slowly ran his eyes along the line of people, and then he saw her.

Laura spotted her at the same time. 'Mummy,' she shrieked loudly, as she pulled her hand away from Hedge's grip and ran off.

Ann McCain ignored the security officer trying to keep people behind the barrier, as she hurled herself towards her daughter. Then they were both locked together, the two of them crying uncontrollably. Laura's mother turned the small girl around in a circle as she held on to her. Several onlookers were staring, and wondering what all the fuss was about, but still the mother and daughter clung to each other, with no attempt to move out of the way of other arriving passengers.

Hedge stood and watched. It was a lovely sight to see. It made the trauma and horror of everything he had recently endured seem worthwhile.

Then he brushed something away from the top of his nose. 'Damned air in here,' he said to himself.

It was the only possible reason he could think of to explain why his eyes had started to fill up with moisture.

Chapter Fifty One

A few days later Hedge met up with his friend again.

'How did the reunion go?' Cole had been unable to come along to return the girl as he had been advised to spend two days in hospital recovering from his injury.

'It was quite emotional, a nice moment to witness.'

Cole laughed. 'In other words you cried like a baby.'

Hedge ignored the remark.

'I'll take that as a yes then,' said Cole.

Once more there was no response from Hedge.

They were standing outside a small, prefabricated building, a few miles from the city of Havana. They had returned to Cuba in an attempt to track down the man known as Uncle Jorge. According to FBI files, he was the mastermind behind the child trafficking operation.

As it happened, finding Jorge had been easy. He was well known in this part of the island, and most of the people they'd asked were only too willing to talk when they saw the large bundle of US dollars in Cole's hand.

Cole had surprised the man when he answered the door to the building a short while ago. He clearly hadn't been expecting any visitors. Jorge now lay flat out on his back in front of them. He was sporting a large, purple-black bruise on the side of his face. Cole had hit him with a thick iron bar, instantly rendering him unconscious. He was an ugly looking guy, and very overweight for his short height. His relaxed double chin looked hideous as he lay on the tarmac. It was drizzling with rain, and his clothes were starting to get wet.

180

'Let's get him ready for his big trip then shall we?' Cole sounded cheerful. He was enjoying the moment.

The box that Jorge had to be placed in rested nearby. As he was a large built man, the whole top of the crate had been removed otherwise they would never have squeezed him in. Cole took a syringe from his shirt pocket. It was wrapped in a clear plastic cover, which he removed carefully. Next he squeezed gently on one end and a small amount of liquid spurted from the needle. He leaned down and pushed this into the prone man's arm.

'That will keep him asleep for the next twenty four hours or so, more than enough time for the crate to reach its destination. You can turn away now if you like. You may not want to see this next bit.' Cole shot a glance towards Hedge, and then he pulled out a short, steel-bladed knife from his trouser pocket. He laid this on the floor close to the Cuban man. Next to that he placed a small pair of wire cutters.

Hedge looked away. In the distance he could see a road which trailed off into a small cluster of hills. The traffic on the road was light, but he tried to focus on the cars and trucks as they passed. It helped to cover the soft, squelching noises he could hear just behind him. After a few minutes Cole had finished his work.

'You can turn round now. It's safe to look.'

Hedge turned back and stared down at Uncle Jorge. 'What the fuck, why is he wrapped in that? And I assume you don't want me to ask where the red stains come from?'

'Best not to I guess.' Cole laughed.

They bundled the heavy body into the crate, sealed it up, and then checked the destination address which was stamped clearly on one side of the wooden box.

Hedge tried to pronounce what was written. 'I've never heard of that place, and I certainly can't read what that scrawl is saying.'

'Most of it is in Arabic. It's a small town on the Syrian and Iraqi border. For the last few years it's been run by a hard-line, fundamentalist religious group. They hate the west and all it stands for. Our friend here will feel right at home there.'

'And what does all this other writing mean?'

'It says enclosed are emergency medical supplies, courtesy of the International Red Crescent. They may be disappointed when the open it, or not. It depends what kind of mood they are in.'

'Are you sure you want to do this?'

Cole looked up. 'I made a promise to the girl's mother.'

Hedge nodded slowly. 'Yes, I guess you did.'

The wooden crate was picked up by a small haulage company based just outside Havana. The driver was a scruffy man, who smoked small cigars constantly. He stank of stale tobacco. Cole gave him the delivery address. The Cuban raised his eyebrows for a brief moment, and then nodded. Cole gave him a large bundle of local currency.

Four hours later, the box was being loaded onto an American military transport plane at Guantanamo Bay. This part of the island is effectively US territory, much to the annoyance of the Cuban government.

A short while after that, the aircraft touched down at Fort Bragg in North Carolina. Although over fifty thousand service personnel are based at this location, nobody at Fort Bragg took the slightest bit of notice as the crate was transferred onto another military cargo flight bound for Iraq.

Cole had spoken to a colleague at MI5 back in London who had made all the necessary calls to his American counterparts. The crate was effectively being transported under diplomatic immunity. No one was allowed to search it, or interfere with its progress in any way.

The crate arrived at a military airport near Baghdad sometime early the following morning local time. The lorry transporting it up to the border area was waiting. The driver looked nervous. He had made the trip several times before but it was still dangerous. Apart from all the unexploded ordnance along the way as a result of the Iraqi wars, there were still many violent factions based in the northern region of the country.

The long journey through this part of Iraq was uneventful. That was until the lorry was approaching the small town of Al Badi. The driver was getting tired. It had been a long day. There was a small crater in the road, possibly as a result of an exploding hand grenade at some point during the war. Too late the driver spotted it. The front wheel of the vehicle dropped into the hole, but the man pulled hard on the steering wheel and luckily managed to keep his vehicle upright.

He had safely returned to the centre of the road. However the front tyre had punctured. The owner of the vehicle hadn't provided all the right tools for a wheel change, so the driver had struggled to fit the spare tyre. He managed it, eventually, but it had taken him four hours. He cursed the owner of the business several times before resuming his journey.

Finally, and with a lot of trepidation, he pulled up in front of the tribal leader's house in the village that was printed on his delivery ticket. Several local men helped him to unload the box. Then, without hanging around for a second longer than he needed to, he jumped back in his lorry, and began the slow return journey to the capital.

The wooden box was still sitting at the side of the road when the head man returned from his afternoon prayers. His head was still spinning from the lively sermon that had just been preached to the faithful. The subject delivered to those gathered had been about the vileness of the western ideology, and how the American's were still supporting the hated Baghdad based regime.

The man was angry. He loathed those other cultures that seemed to want to destroy his way of thinking. He despised the ideals of the rich nations on this earth. Freedom of speech, women being equal to men, smart phones, and chewing gum. He hated it all.

'A plague on all those disbelievers, he muttered to himself.

A small crowd of men had gathered around the crate. With a nod of approval from the leader, they started to prise off the lid. There were shrieks of surprise and delight as a few eager heads looked into the box.

The head man barged his way through the crowd. Medical supplies did not usually draw this much merriment from his men. As he looked inside the crate, he gasped, and slowly a smile spread across his face. The fat man looking up at him had blood encrusted round his mouth, as his tongue had been cut out. There were small, red stains also at the end of both of his arms, this as a result of all of his fingers being cut off.

Therefore he could not explain either verbally, or in writing, why he was draped in a large American flag. The red, white, and blue colours of the star spangled banner screamed their abuse up from the depth of the gloom inside the crate.

The leader looked up to the sky above. His mouth opened to reveal a set of blackened teeth, and he shouted out commands at the top of his voice.

'Fetch the women. Tell them to sharpen their small knives. We have a fat rabbit to skin.'

Chapter Fifty Two

The man known as Uncle Jorge was dragged out of the crate. He was terrified, and confused. The pain in his mouth was unbearable, and he couldn't move his fingers. They were completely numb. So were his arms. The men pulling at him were talking in a strange language. His head suddenly spun sideways as a fist landed on his jaw. Then he was being kicked and punched all over. The bright sunlight was blinding, so he shut his eyes tightly, and curled up his body on the dusty ground.

As he lay there, soaking up the kicks, he became aware of a tall man shouting. Then the impacts to his body suddenly stopped. Next, he heard the voices of women. They were laughing, almost shrieking. He couldn't make out if they were terrified or delighted.

The women picked him up between them. It wasn't easy as he was a big man. It took several of them. They hauled him away down the street, turning off the main road after a hundred yards or so. There was a large area of waste ground behind a closed down factory unit. They dumped the man on the ground, and started to strip off his clothes. One of the women produced a plastic mallet and some short metal stakes. She knocked them into the hard ground in roughly the shape of a square. They tied Jorge's hands and feet to the metal pegs.

The Cuban was now lying completely naked, face up, with his arms and legs outstretched. As much as he pulled against the ropes holding him, it didn't do any good. They had secured him well. It was a hot day, and the sky was cloudless. The sun beat down on his exposed skin. He started to sweat.

The village women were all dressed in black. Their faces and hands were gnarled from years of hard toil out in the heat. They were laughing and chattering constantly, exposing their black teeth and yellow gums.

Suddenly the mood changed. Four of the group came and kneeled in front of the exposed body of Jorge. Each of them clasped a small knife. The blades were thin and wafer-like, and looked like they had been honed to perfection.

Jorge cried out. It was a fearful scream, muted somewhat by the swollen stub of his tongue. Again he tried to pull away from the ropes holding him down, but to no avail.

One of the women leaned forward, and with a smooth motion of her hand, she ran the blade of the knife along his chest. It was an amazing sight to behold. The skill of the old lady was incredible. A thin sliver of the man's skin came away just as if she was peeling a potato. She picked up the piece of skin, rolled it up in the palm of her hand, and then dropped it into her own mouth. The other women hooted with laughter as she slowly chewed on the man's flesh.

Jorge shrieked as he felt the blade running across him. He looked down at the damaged area and let out a long wailing sound. The area of missing skin didn't bleed, but it quickly turned bright red. Then the other women joined in. Four knives were now scraping along his body. Within a few minutes most of the skin had been removed from his chest, stomach, shoulders, and the tops of his arms. Most of the surface of his body was now red and raw. In a few patches the heat of the sun had started to make his flesh bubble slightly.

The man was in agony. Any small movement that he made simply stretched the exposed flesh which resulted in horrendous bolts of pain. His wailing was loud, and non-stop. Such was the noise he was making that the men folk of the village, who had been told to leave the women to get on with their task, couldn't resist coming to see what was going on. They gathered around him now. A space opened up as the village leader pushed his way through.

The old man laughed out loud. Then he clicked his fingers towards a young boy and shouted something. The boy ran off, but came back almost immediately clutching a small, muslin bag. The leader dipped his hand into the bag, grabbed a handful of the fine crystalline substance inside, and started to sprinkle this over the exposed flesh of the Cuban.

The man on the ground screeched at the top of his voice. His screams would have been heard a long way off. The effect of the salt touching his raw flesh was unbearable. He writhed in agony. Much of the awful noise he was making was being drowned out by the hysterical laughter of the crowd around him.

The village leader waved to the men gathered around, and shouted out more commands. Slowly the men drifted away, leaving the women to finish the job. They still had the man's legs to strip. Then there was the more delicate work. The face, neck and feet would be more difficult. The final touches, the man's penis and scrotum, would complete the job. The men would certainly be keen to see the finished product.

Sometimes it could take several days for a person to eventually die, or they may only last a few hours. It really depended on the individual. Either way, the old women didn't really care.

They knelt down with their knives and carried on with their handiwork.

Chapter Fifty Three

The flight back to London left Miami International airport at three o'clock in the afternoon. With adjustment for the time difference, Hedge and Cole would arrive home early the following morning.

They had travelled back to Florida from Cuba as the FBI had formally requested that they be debriefed after their recent trip to Jordan. John Hughes had organised the meeting personally. It had been a brief conversation. Hughes hadn't made many notes, or asked them to go into much detail. He did though seem interested in a few loose ends, as he called them.

'My sources tell me that a foreign national, a woman called Olga, was found naked in a warehouse at around the same time as your visit. She was given a hundred and twenty lashes in the main public square in Amman for inappropriate conduct. Do you know anything about that?'

Cole shrugged. Hedge shook his head.

Hughes looked at them both for a moment longer and then glanced back down at his notes.

'We have been following a man known as Jorge for some time now. He may, or may not, be involved in the child trafficking that we are investigating. His last known whereabouts was near Havana in Cuba. The guy has completely disappeared, vanished into thin air. Would the pair of you happen to know anything about that?'

Cole looked astonished. 'Vanished you say. That's amazing. And you FBI guys are such professionals. How does someone just simply disappear when you are keeping such a close eye on them?'

Hughes ignored the remark. He stared at Hedge. Once again Hedge responded with a shake of his head.

'And you don't happen to have come across a well built man called Max?' Hughes looked like he was beginning to get annoyed.

'Max, no I don't think so.' Cole looked genuinely intrigued. 'Who is he?'

Hughes looked Cole directly in the eyes, trying to work out if he was being given the run-around. 'We believe he is a hired thug working for the traffickers. He's a big, muscle-bound guy. His weapon of choice is a baseball bat.'

'Sounds like the man the witnesses described on the bus in Gainesville.' Hedge's response seemed genuine enough.

Hughes studied him for a moment before replying. 'We found him dead yesterday. He was tied up lying flat out on his back in a warehouse on the outskirts of Miami. Cause of death was severe burns to over seventy percent of his body. The pathologist said he would have passed away in agony. Do you know anything about that?'

Hedge shrugged his shoulders. 'No I don't I'm afraid. Just as well really, it's sounds quite horrific.'

Hughes turned to face Cole. 'What about you?'

'Nothing to do with me, although it sounds like the guy deserved everything he got. No, sorry, can't help you with that. I wouldn't know how to operate a blowtorch anyway.'

'Who said anything about a blowtorch?' Hughes snapped back at him. 'I didn't mention that. How did you know about the blowtorch?'

'You said that was how he was burnt.'

'I never mentioned a blowtorch.'

'You did, a minute ago, when you told us about finding this Max guy.' Cole turned towards Hedge. 'He mentioned it, didn't he?'

Hedge nodded in agreement. 'You definitely mentioned a blowtorch. I heard it clearly.'

Hughes looked at Hedge and then turned to stare at Cole. He looked confused, but there was also a deep suspicion showing on his face.

'If I find out that you guys are fucking with me, then you will be in deep trouble. I'm personally taking you to the airport. I want to make sure you both get on a plane back to England.'

He concluded the meeting and then escorted them out of the building, telling them to wait near the main entrance. He pulled up a short while later. Hedge jumped into the front of the Buick Lacrosse, while Cole sat in the back. He was in the seat directly behind the FBI man. Hughes turned and dropped his briefcase, his coat, and his handgun on the vacant back seat.

'That's a nice piece,' said Cole. He recognised the handgun immediately. It was a Sig Sauer 9mm. 'Good choice of weapon for someone in your line of work.'

Hughes grunted his agreement, and then pulled out into the stream of traffic heading out of the city.

Arriving at the airport, Hughes pulled the car into the short term parking area. It was a multi-storey building and he drove all the way to the top.

'I like to keep out of the way of everyone else,' he explained.

'Good idea.' Cole agreed.

Hughes pulled the Buick into a free space. There were plenty of them to choose as no one else was about.

'There's just one thing I can't understand,' said Cole. He spoke slowly and deliberately. 'You know, when I saw that list of payments made from the Cuban bank account, the one my London contact gave me.'

Hughes had turned off the vehicle's ignition. He sat bolt upright, still in the driver's seat in front of Cole.

'You did mention that. Yes, what of it?'

'Can you explain why your name was on it? There was a payment transfer to a Mr. J Hughes with a Miami bank account. I assume the J stands for John?'

Cole couldn't see it, but the FBI man's face had gone as white as a ghost. 'I..I can explain that. I... It's...You see..'

Hughes was struggling to speak coherently. Hedge sat quietly in the seat next to him, not sure how this was going to end.

'Let's hear the explanation then.' Cole's voice was confident. He knew he had the man in a corner. 'Actually, to be honest, I don't give a shit about what you say. I'm bored with all this now. I just want to go home.'

There was a thunderous bang in the back of the car. The bullet from the Sig passed through the driver's seat, shattered Hughes's spinal column as it passed through his body, and exited just above his stomach. Blood, bone and small pieces of flesh were splattered across the front of the vehicle.

Cole put the gun back down on the seat next to him, and carefully wiped it with the dead man's coat sleeve. Hedge turned round in his seat to look back at his friend. His eyes seemed to be demanding some sort of explanation.

Cole looked back at him. He looked totally remorseless.

'I made a promise to Laura's mother.'

Epilogue

Andy Adcock was the senior boy who was bullying Hedge, and who dropped his friend Baker down at stairwell at Upperdale College. Well as it happened, it wasn't the last time that drinking excessive alcohol would land him in trouble. Almost a year after finishing school, he was arrested for drinking and driving close to his home in Cambridge. He had been out partying with friends, and should have taken a taxi home, but he thought he would drive himself instead. The driver and passenger of the Audi A4 he hit as he swerved onto the wrong side of the road both survived the head on collision. So too did Adcock. The four year old boy in the back of the Audi didn't. His neck broke as his head was jerked forwards in the impact. Adcock was sentenced to five years in prison. The protestors outside the court thought he should have got longer, much longer.

Once the task of skinning the body of Uncle Jorge had been completed, the village leader and some of his men came to view him one last time. The Cuban pleaded to be put out of his misery. The pain was too much to bear. His request fell on deaf ears. One of the villagers had found a second bag of salt, and Jorge received another liberal sprinkling of the stuff all over his body. It is told that the screams resulting from that were heard over three miles away, although that may be a slight exaggeration. Several days later the body of Uncle Jorge was found to have been almost completely devoured by wild dogs. It is not known for certain whether he was still alive or not when the animals began their feast.

The doctor in Amman who had agreed to perform the operations on the two girls was prosecuted for malpractice. The court decided that he was guilty and the judge sent him to prison for ten years. The terrible conditions in the jail, coupled with the shame he had brought to his family, were too much for him to bear. Just three weeks after the trial, he was found in his cell with both his wrists slashed. He had bled to death. He was a wealthy man by Jordanian standards, and in his will he left a substantial sum of money to a young girl called Hala. She was to use the inheritance in order to make the remaining few years of her life as comfortable as possible.

Laura was one of the lucky few. She was found and returned to her mother. Many of the young children stolen were never seen again. It was lucky that Ann, her mother, had friends in high places. Otherwise there may not have been the resources available to track her down. The British government had to assist as it could not afford the publicity of a scandal. The Treasury Minister at the centre of the scandal was so relieved to see Laura safely back with her mother, that he decided to take full responsibility for the child. So he started formal proceedings in order to be recognised as the father. There was a lot of paperwork to be completed, but he could afford to hire a good lawyer. The process failed at the final hurdle. The official DNA test came back negative. There was no match between him and the girl. As it turned out, he could not possibly have been Laura's father.

As usual, Hedge's world had been turned completely upside down by the latest adventure with Cole. He was looking forward to getting back to normal life. But then, although the danger and uncertainty frightened him terribly, was there an element of it that he enjoyed? He pondered that thought for a while. No, he didn't think so. That would be ridiculous. Nobody in their right mind would want to be in situations where bad people wanted to do you serious harm. He let the thought drift away.

He hoped that he would meet his friend Cole again soon.

Somehow it seemed quite likely.

THE END

Books by Kevin Bradley

The Palindrome Cult
(Hedge & Cole / Book 1)
"A cracking good read, fast and furious, unputdownable"

The Terminate Code
(Hedge & Cole / Book 2)
"A fantastic story, breathtaking and full of intrigue, unforgettable"

The Transamerica Cell
(Hedge & Cole / Book 3)
"A gripping, tense thriller, you'll be on the edge of your seat"

The Cuba Cage
(Hedge & Cole / Book 4)
"A shockingly good novel, full of terror and suspense"

Bully Boys
(Hedge & Cole / Supplement)
"A brutal and sadistic account of boarding school life"

The Hedge & Cole Thriller Series (Books 1-4)
(Hedge & Cole / The Collection)
"A 4 book set of gripping, action adventure novels"

Review

If you liked this book, then please go to Amazon and leave it a good review.

I send you my best wishes.

Kevin Bradley

The following are the opening two chapters of the 3rd book in the Hedge & Cole series.

The Transamerica Cell by Kevin Bradley

Chapter One

Seth Harper saw the three men walking towards him.

He knew they were coming for him, he had been expecting it. One of the men had the fingers of his right hand extended out in front of him. He was pulling on a set of brass knuckles. These were also often referred to as knuckledusters. This simple type of weapon is used in hand to hand combat, and is usually made of a heavy metal. The idea being that when used effectively, the victim would sustain maximum tissue damage, with the increased likelihood of bone fracture occurring.

Seth reached into his jacket pocket and pulled out his cell phone. He looked at the display. The first contact on his list read simply 'Brother Joe.' He touched his finger on the phone next to that name and held the phone to his ear.

The call was answered on the second ring.

'Hi Seth, I can't talk now, I'm out on patrol.'

'Joe, I need help. They're coming for me.' There was panic in his voice.

'Seth. Who is coming for you? Where are you?'

'I'm down in the Pacific Beach area, just off Grand Avenue. I need help, quick ...'

The call went dead.

'Seth. Seth. Hello. Hello. Shit, he's gone.'

Joe Harper turned the steering wheel hard left. The patrol car lurched and spun round.

'We need to head over to Pacific Beach. My brother is in some kind of trouble.'

Joe's partner looked across at him. 'Are you going to call it in?'

'No. No need for that. Let's see what he's up to first. Knowing Seth, it will all be about nothing,' replied Joe.

His partner nodded. 'Fine, let's go.'

Joe stamped his foot on the accelerator pedal and the car jumped forward. At the same time, he flicked a button on the side of the steering wheel. The blue light on the top of the patrol car began flashing. That should be enough, he thought. No need for the siren just yet.

The first of the three men to reach Seth was a tall guy, with a crooked looking face. His left eye had a long-healed scar just underneath it, and his nose looked like it had been broken several times.

The man grabbed the cell phone off Seth, and threw it to the floor. He had heavy boots on his feet, and so when he stamped on the handset, the front screen shattered instantly.

The other two had now arrived, and all three of them grabbed hold of Seth. Together they dragged him into a nearby alley. As he was being pulled along, Seth stumbled and fell to the ground. His three assailants gathered around him, and began kicking at his body. The man wearing the brass knuckles leaned down and directed a strong punch at the base of Seth's ribcage, on his left side. There was a loud cracking noise as one of his ribs broke.

'Did you hear that,' the man shouted. 'What a beautiful sound.'

Seth screamed. A sharp pain ran down his side. He was lying on his front, with his back exposed, desperately trying to protect his head with his hands.'

'Enough. That's enough for now,' the tall man shouted.

His two accomplices stood back. Seth lay motionless on the ground.

'So where is my money?' the tall man said.

'I don't have it, but I'll get it soon. I promise.' Seth said softly. He wiped his hand across his face, and cleared some of the blood away. It was dribbling out of his nose, and running down his face.

'Not good enough,' said the tall man. 'I need it today.'

'I can't get it today. Give me a week. I promise I'll have it in a week.'

'I need it today.'

'Please. One week. Please.'

The tall man swore as he stood up. He looked quickly up and down the alley. There was no one else about. He reached inside his black, leather jacket and pulled something out. He held the weapon in his outstretched right hand, and turned it so that the sunlight glistened off the eight inch blade.

He nodded towards his two colleagues. One of them smiled as he dropped his knees onto the back of the man lying on the floor. Seth was now pinned down and couldn't move. The other attacker walked over and kicked Seth's ankles outwards, so that his legs ended up splayed apart.

'This is your last chance. I need what you owe me now, today. Hopefully this will get your brain working out how you are going to achieve that.'

The tall man swung the knife at Seth's backside. The blade of the weapon sank into his left buttock, penetrating to around five inches. The tall man felt his hand vibrate as the blade bounced off a piece of bone somewhere deep inside the soft flesh.

Seth screamed aloud. The pain inside his buttock was intense, even more so when he felt the steel of the blade scraping along one of his bones. He couldn't stop crying out. The steel was still in his flesh, and it felt like a thousand sharp needles had been pushed into his body.

One of the men took off his woollen hat, and held it over Seth's mouth to try and lessen the noise he was making.

The tall man stood up. He left the blade buried in Seth's backside. He pushed his heavy boot against the handle of the knife, making it move back and forth.

Seth screamed even louder. Dark red blood was seeping out from the wound.

'Do you have any fresh ideas yet on getting me my money?'

'Please, give me some time. Just a few days, please.' Seth spoke slowly, and quietly, with the words coming out in between deep, painful breaths.

The tall man shook his head in resignation.

He leaned down, and with one swift action he pulled the knife out of Seth's buttock. There was a brief sucking noise as the blade came free. Seth's body convulsed and a long, piercing howl came from his throat.

The tall man looked at the blood coated blade. He pulled his arm back slightly.

'You leave me no choice then,' he said.

Chapter Two

'Hey, what are you up to? Leave him alone.'

Robin Taylor didn't consider himself to be a particularly brave man, but when he saw the three guys standing over someone lying on the ground, he decided to try and intervene.

'I've called the police,' Robin lied.

He was hoping that the three attackers would turn and run, but they didn't. Instead they just looked directly at him as he approached them. The man on the floor was moaning softly. Other than that, he lay still and inert.

The tallest man in the group was nearest to Robin. He turned to face the approaching stranger. As he did so, Robin caught sight of the menacing looking weapon he was holding in his hand. The blade looked long, and was covered in a sticky, red liquid.

Robin stopped walking. He stood motionless, his eyes unblinking, as he stared at the knife.

'And who exactly are you?' said the tall man. His voice was quiet, but his throat sounded hoarse, almost like he had a bad cold, or the flu. He was still gripping the weapon in his right hand.

'I've called the police. They told me that they are on their way.' Robin felt very vulnerable now, so close to the three men. He couldn't stop staring at the knife.

'I'm sure you have,' said the tall man. He was sneering, but the look that he gave Robin was chilling.

It was a hot day, almost ninety degrees Robin estimated. As it was lunch time, the streets in this part of San Diego were quiet. Most people had headed off to get something to eat, or to find somewhere cooler to pass the next couple of hours.

Robin didn't know what he should do next. With hindsight, he was now wishing that he hadn't got involved in this situation. He should have just walked on by. His wife and two young daughters would be waiting for him in the department store just around the next block. That was where they had planned to meet up for something to eat.

His thoughts were suddenly interrupted as the tall man let out a loud cry. Robin was startled, and automatically took a step back. The man had raised his right hand, the one holding the knife, high up in the air. He brought it down rapidly, catching those watching by surprise. As the weapon came down, the man turned slightly, leaned down lower, and plunged the eight inch blade into the back of the head of the man lying on the ground.

The knife was sharp, and it was forced right through the victim's head. The handle of the weapon was pushed up against the soft, fleshy part at the back of the skull, just above the man's neck. The point of the blade ended up coming out of the front of the head, so that it was just visible between the top of the man's nose and his left eyeball.

The body on the floor wriggled and shook for a few moments, and then it was still.

The tall man threw his head back and laughed. 'Has anyone got any headache tablets? This guy has a terrible need for some.'

The other two men also started to laugh. One of them kicked out and aimed his foot straight at the face of the body on the ground.

His boot caught the man in the mouth, snapping off several of his front teeth. There was no reaction. The body on the ground was beyond any kind of response now.

Robin couldn't believe what he had just witnessed. He was horrified, and in a state of shock. He took a few paces backwards, trying to get himself away from the murder scene. The three men moved towards him, the tall man at the front, smiling.

Suddenly, the smile had gone. It was replaced with a look of panic. The alley they were in was reasonably well lit, certainly not dark. Even so, the blue light bouncing off the alley walls was clearly visible, just for a split second, as the patrol car slowly drove past.

The three men turned and ran. They headed off down the alley, away from where Robin was standing. After some thirty yards, they turned right into an adjoining passage, and completely disappeared from sight.

Robin was still terrified, but his first thought was to try and help the man lying on the ground. He ran over and knelt next to the body. There was no movement. Blood was pouring from the man's head. Robin tried to pull the knife out, but it was stuck fast. He tried to wipe the sticky, red liquid off his fingers, but all he succeeded in doing was staining his clothes.

It was hopeless. The man lay completely still. He must be dead, Robin thought.

He turned around, just in time to see the police car backing up the street. It had obviously driven past the alley, but something had attracted the suspicion of the officers in the car. The vehicle stopped and Officer Joe Harper opened the driver's door and jumped out.

'What's going on here?' Joe could see the man lying on the ground.

As he entered the alley, he pulled his Glock 22 handgun from its holster. He must have been about ten yards from the body, when he suddenly recognised who it was.

'Seth,' he shouted, as he ran forward.

Joe stopped when he reached his brother. He raised his pistol towards Robin as he shouted his orders.

'Turn around slowly, so that you are facing away from me. Move towards the wall and place your arms above your head.'

Robin tried to speak, but no words came from his mouth. He was still in a state of shock.

'Do it now,' shouted Joe.

Robin turned, and did as he was told. His hands were covered in blood still, something Joe noticed as he turned to focus his attention on the body in front of him.

'Oh my god,' Joe said quietly as he tried to find a pulse in Seth's neck.

Joe was a seasoned police officer. He had seen many dead bodies in his time. Some of them had been shot, a few occasionally drowned, and many of them had stab wounds. But this was different. This was his brother, his own flesh and blood.

He tried to focus, but it wasn't easy. There were tears running down his face. He pressed a button on his radio, and called for an ambulance. He knew it was too late for that, but that's what you did in a situation like this.

Joe stood up. He looked down at the body of his brother. His heart was pounding in his ears, and his eyes were stinging. His mind was racing. But most of all, his rage was building to an impossible level.

'Who the hell has done this to my kid brother?' he asked himself.

He looked across the alley at the man holding his hands above his head.

His red hands.

Printed in Great Britain
by Amazon